## Released from the icy clutches of the sea

There was only the sound of the waves, and harsh breathing. Barrabas, Nanos and Hayes slowly gathered strength and sat up to look into the faces of Lee, Billy Two and Liam, expecting to see welcoming smiles for the heroes of the deep.

Instead they looked as though the battle had been lost.

"What the hell's the matter with you? We got what we were looking for," Barrabas said.

In answer, O'Toole flipped one of the bodies over with his foot. The face was a mass of scarred flesh and white bones.

"Crabs," Lee said. "Crustaceans will do this every time."

Suddenly they were distracted by a change in the constant noise of the jets overhead. One of the Foxbats had broken formation and was making a missile run straight at them.

The SOBs pounded the deck toward the missile emplacements. Before they could man their positions, they realized it was too late.

They were sitting ducks.

# SOBs
## SOLDIERS OF BARRABAS

#1 The Barrabas Run
#2 The Plains of Fire
#3 Butchers of Eden
#4 Show No Mercy
#5 Gulag War
#6 Red Hammer Down
#7 River of Flesh
#8 Eye of the Fire
#9 Some Choose Hell
#10 Vultures of the Horn
#11 Agile Retrieval
#12 Jihad
#13 No Sanctuary
#14 Red Vengeance
#15 Death Deal
#16 Firestorm U.S.A.
#17 Point Blank
#18 Sakhalin Breakout
#19 Skyjack
#20 Alaska Deception

# SOBs
## SOLDIERS OF BARRABAS

# ALASKA DECEPTION

## JACK HILD

## A GOLD EAGLE BOOK FROM
# W🌐RLDWIDE

TORONTO • NEW YORK • LONDON • PARIS
AMSTERDAM • STOCKHOLM • HAMBURG
ATHENS • MILAN • TOKYO • SYDNEY

First edition September 1987

ISBN 0-373-61620-1

Special thanks and acknowledgment to
Jack Garside for his contribution to this work.

Printed in Canada

**1**

## Late September

It was night. Moscow smelled of burning leaves. A brisk wind carried swirling remnants of a painfully short autumn around the dim streetlights and under the eaves of buildings around Marx Prospekt and Dzerzhinsky Square. The few Muscovites on the streets were bundled against the first chill warnings of a long winter to come. Most sat at home, watching propaganda on television or reading the state newspapers.

At 2 Dzerzhinsky Square, in a small, sparsely furnished office off a back corridor at the headquarters of the dreaded Komitet Gosudarstvennoi Bezopasnosti, Colonel Alexi Petrov sat facing a foreigner. They were alone. A picture of the grim-faced first secretary stared down at them from otherwise bare walls. A bottle of vodka and two glasses were the only articles on the scarred desk between them. The Frenchman had asked for Pernod and ice, but the Russian colonel had scorned the request, producing the national drink and two glasses.

The small room smelled of soap and lye from the swabbing it received every night. Slowly the faint odor of vodka took over.

The setting wasn't Petrov's usual style. As the deputy director of the most secret KGB department, the Executive Action Department of the First Chief Directorate, known as Department V, responsible for sabotage and *mokrie dela*, "wet affairs," he was accustomed to better surroundings. And it was evident he wasn't pleased with the assignment.

The Frenchman opposite him was short, compared to the tall muscular colonel. He was also fat, myopic and disheveled. It was obvious to the colonel's nose that the man hadn't bathed for days. It was also becoming evident that he couldn't hold his vodka.

"You are a pig, Beaudreau," Petrov said with total disdain. "It's not my choice to work with you. Now, what the hell are you planning and what do you want from us?"

"It has the blessing of your chief." Beaudreau grinned foolishly, sipping vodka between his yellowed teeth.

Petrov loathed the slob sitting across the desk. The job he'd been given was an albatross around his neck. "Don't be too sure of that," Petrov said scornfully. "We've heard only a brief outline of your plan. The general will not move without my agreement."

"Best chance you've had to blame someone else— maybe hit the Americans on their own soil," the

Frenchman slurred through uncertain lips. "Pick some targets and we'll blame it on Greenpeace."

"Not so fast," Petrov commanded. "I know you were with Greenpeace. I know you and some friends think you have a score to settle with them. Now let's have details. Is the French government already paying you?"

"I spit on my own government. Cheap bastards!"

"They want revenge for all the trouble over the bombing of the *Rainbow Warrior* in Auckland harbor. That's what this is all about?"

"They've been ordered to pay seven million in reparations. Appealing the decision." He held the soiled glass so tightly that his knuckles turned white. "My best friend was killed in the bombing," Beaudreau spit out. "It was as much Greenpeace's fault as the bloody government's. And I'm going to make the bastards look bad. I'm going to get them, finally."

"So why work for the ones who planted the bomb?"

"I said they were cheap. I didn't say they were wrong. It was the stubbornness of the Greenpeace bastards who killed Raymond. They pushed too much as usual. Damn them! I left the movement because they were too stubborn—too damned sure they were right all the time. And they were chicken. No real action. They should have used force as I recommended." He reached for the vodka bottle with a shaking hand and filled his glass.

"So you took money from the French to discredit Greenpeace. How much? What do they expect?"

"Not enough," Beaudreau muttered in his heavily accented English. Petrov's French was almost non-existent and Beaudreau's Russian was worse, so they used English as their common language. "They left the plan to me," he went on. "I'm going to hire an old trawler, paint her to look like *Rainbow Warrior*, and blow something up. I haven't decided what yet."

Petrov was stubborn. "How much?" he asked again.

"One-half million American dollars. What the hell can I do with a half-million?"

Petrov sat almost erect as he downed the last of his drink. He wondered if he wanted his people to get involved at all. A plan was forming in his agile brain, but it would have to be handled with extreme care. Maybe the general was thinking along the same lines and Petrov wouldn't have to commit himself. "So you came to us for more money?" he asked.

"Right. More money," Beaudreau slurred.

"You've already been paid by the French. They're the ones who want to make Greenpeace look bad after all the publicity about the Auckland bombing. Why should we get involved?"

"What they offered me covers expenses. I could hire a rusty old hulk and its crew, make it look like the Greenpeace ship and attack a target. But what's left for me? Nothing."

"A true terrorist. You want it both ways," Petrov said with disgust. "I'll have to talk it over with my chief." He downed his vodka in one gulp and poured another. "I hope your god thinks kindly of you and your plan, Beaudreau, or you may see him sooner than you planned."

Beaudreau drank slowly as Petrov watched. The Frenchman had been allowed into the Soviet Union because the chief of the First Directorate wanted to examine the possibility of using him.

Petrov knew the French had already paid for Beaudreau's wild plan to discredit Greenpeace. As the slob opposite him said, the French were both cheap and stupid: they paid Beaudreau and his group a half-million American and didn't direct his actions. Beaudreau could, and probably would, make a mess of it at that price, and the French would be blamed. Petrov had anticipated most of the details before talking to Beaudreau and didn't think much of the scheme. But he had talked earlier with the chief, and the old fool had seen some merit in using the Frenchman. He had charged Petrov with the job of examining the whole situation carefully.

"You don't even realize the scope of your plan, do you?" he asked the Frenchman. "All you can think of is petty revenge because your Greenpeace pals were too pacifist for your taste?"

"And it was their fault Ray got killed."

"One thing I'll give them is guts," Petrov said. "I've seen them work a whaling ship."

"I've lived and worked with them, and I don't agree. No balls. They rush around shouting, dropping pamphlets. Bunch of scared shits," Jacques Beaudreau said, his fat arms cradling his head to keep it from falling on the desk. His stained blue shirt and faded jeans were in blatant contrast to Petrov's immaculate military-style Savile Row suit.

Petrov sat looking at the fat man with distaste. He was silent for a long time, then spoke as if to himself. "I admit your damned Greenpeace has been like a swarm of locusts to us," he finally said, pouring another vodka for himself with a steady hand. "They've harassed our whaling fleets, sent thousands of balloons filled with pamphlets to our citizens to discredit our fishing practices. Dozens of nuisance schemes. Always underfoot."

"Lots of your people hate Greenpeace, big man."

"You found my director's weak spot!" Petrov slammed his fist on the table. The bottle jumped, and he caught it before it toppled. "He can't stand to have an enemy go unpunished. He's been looking for a way to get back at them. But we could be overreacting. Your plan is too obvious. Everybody knows Greenpeace is nonviolent." Petrov scowled as he poured yet another drink from the almost empty bottle. The fiery liquid didn't seem to affect him.

"Going soft, are you, Colonel?" Beaudreau taunted, his head unsteady on his shoulders.

"Damn you!" Petrov shouted, lashing out and knocking the Frenchman to the floor. "If your scheme backfires, you'll wish you'd never seen my country."

Petrov walked around the table, stood over the besotted Greenpeace radical, his dark brown hair disheveled by the blow he'd thrown. He put down his glass and walked to the door with a steady gait, straightening his coat and combing his hair with long, manicured fingers.

Beaudreau was sprawled on the floor, his mouth agape, his eyes closed. He hadn't heard a word.

Petrov left the fat Frenchman where he lay and walked along a dimly lit corridor to the offices of the heads of directorates. Even at this hour, guards patrolled the corridors, and his identification was checked three times before he reached his chief's office. It was after midnight. The general had told him to report back no matter the hour.

He didn't like it at all. If they made it look as though the French were behind it, they couldn't hope to make it work more than once. One raid quickly in and out. And they'd have to rely on fools like Beaudreau. He didn't want any part of it, but he had no choice. A fact of life in Russia. Even those with power had few choices that were entirely their own.

GENERAL BORIS MESMEROF sat behind a massive carved-oak desk in a corner office on the top floor of KGB headquarters. It was ten times the size of the room where Beaudreau lay, and in direct contrast, it was decorated with colorful tapestries and paintings worthy of showing in Moscow's National Gallery. It smelled of freshly waxed wood and the scent of fresh-cut flowers. The broad windows looked down on Dzerzhinsky's statue, a windswept likeness of the Komitet's founder.

Mesmerof had plotted and fought his way from a collective farm to head the First Chief Directorate of the world's largest intelligence agency. He was responsible for all Soviet clandestine operations abroad not handled by the GRU, the Soviet military intelligence.

The long years of infighting within the party had taken their toll on Mesmerof. Apart from the effects of mental anguish—the cynicism and constant fear—his physical condition was deplorable. He had gone to soft fat, lost all his hair and, through the excesses available to the elite, overindulged. He was a candidate for bypass surgery, a fact known only to his doctor and to himself.

One of his best men was Colonel Alexi Petrov, who now stood in front of the desk at rigid attention. Mesmerof liked Petrov and had put him in charge of the most secret department in the Komitet. He'd been grooming the younger man as his successor.

Like all the new ones fighting their way to the top, Petrov had his weakness. In Mesmerof's opinion, he had a stubborn streak. When Mesmerof had been that age he wouldn't have dared question his chief.

"Sit down, Alexi," he said, pointing to an open bottle of twelve-year-old Johnny Walker in front of him. Unlike his peers, he had never cared for vodka. "Take some Scotch."

He watched his tall and handsome deputy sit and pour with a steady hand.

"What did you think of Beaudreau?" the general asked.

"You were wise not to see him yourself. An opportunist, but not very bright. Without our guidance, he will make a mess of it."

"What do you suggest?" the old warrior asked.

"We set up the plan, train the people ourselves and pay him as little as possible," Petrov said.

"I would like to use him to hit the American oil fields in Alaska."

Petrov sat immobilized by shock for a moment. He should have known the general would come up with something. His own plan had been daring, but not as radical.

"I don't like the idea of hitting an American target on American soil," he said. "We'd cut off their oil supply from Alaska, maybe destroy a major oil field. That's a plus, but they wouldn't be fooled for long, and their response could be devastating."

"We'll have to make sure it looks like the French are behind it. And we'll have to hit them more than once to deprive them of Alaska oil."

"More than once? Impossible! Couldn't we go for another target? Believe me, General, this is only going to work once because the real Greenpeace people will be able to prove it wasn't them."

"We're going to hit the American oil installations. We'll strike as many times as we have to, and to hell with the real Greenpeace people." The general reached for the bottle and filled his own glass again. "The crew will be Beaudreau's people, trained by us. The ships will fly the French flag."

"I don't like it. If they're caught, they'll talk."

The general ignored him. "We'll need raiding parties. What about the dissident Eskimo at the Chukchi Peninsula? They've been a pain in the ass for years. We can use them as assault forces, set up a base there and strike in the spring."

"Train all winter? Have you ever been to Chukchi? It's worse than Siberia."

"And you, my dear Petrov, will supervise the training."

The younger man was stunned for a few seconds, then he regained control. He reached for the bottle, poured a full glass and downed half the brown liquid in one gulp. "I suggest we supply the ships," he finally said. "We can wire them for electronic demolition at any time." He emptied the glass. "We pay the Frenchman very little," he went on. "We're supplying the ships, and he's been paid once already." He was not exactly enamored of the plan, but he knew his involvement was inevitable. "I still don't like striking American soil. Have you the agreement of the first secretary on this?"

"You will not tell me how to do my job, Alexi Petrov!" the older man shouted, pounding on the desk. "I will tell him when it is all set up. We'll see how it looks in the spring." He sat like an old Buddha, round and smiling enigmatically. "We will bring in the ships and crews when everything else is set up. Paint the rainbow colors at the last minute—maybe even at sea. We will hit and sneak away. If we are about to be overtaken, you can use your electronic detonators. Of course, that means you will be on the scene." He smiled again, his yellowed teeth making a rare appearance.

"It will be one hell of a winter," Petrov observed, almost to himself.

"Make it work, Alexi. Put it all together and make it work. I want the Americans to lose their Alaska oil."

ON THE WAY TO HIS APARTMENT, Petrov sat back in his limousine and thought about the past few hours. He shivered involuntarily. The Frenchman would be running the show once they left Russian soil. It was a weakness he couldn't live with. He'd have to plant some of his people in the crew and find a way to be close to the action.

The dissident Chukchi Eskimo could be trained for their task through the winter, but he'd have to find a way to make sure they wouldn't reveal anything if captured. That was a tall order.

Hell! This one had too many holes in it. Attacking the American mainland was risky, even under a French flag. The French had been foolhardy enough to give Beaudreau a free hand.

His mind was awash with doubt. But maybe it would work. If it didn't, he foresaw American ships and planes surrounding Alaska and shooting at everything in sight. It could even be worse. It could mean the unleashing of ICBMs.

The first priority was to make sure no one talked—after destroying the oil fields. Damn! He began to wonder if his chief was going senile. Each successive job the old man gave him seemed more risky. Or was the fault with him? Was he going soft? Maybe the old man was squeezing him out.

He'd have to make this one work. The general was sick. He didn't have much time left. Maybe this would be his last wild scheme before he, Petrov, took over the Directorate. He let that thought sustain him as the big black car pulled into the underground parking entrance. The old bastard might be trying to squeeze him out, but it could work in reverse.

## 2

**Late May**

Twenty-knot northwesterlies tore along the coast out of the Chukchi Sea, pushing the remnants of the spring breakup seaward in miniature icebergs the size of rowboats. The air was crisp and fresh, free of pollution or the smell of decay.

The new base at Inchoun, a remote fishing village on the northeast coast of Chukchi Peninsula, had been hell to build through the winter, but it was finally finished.

The Northern Command of the army had been seconded by Colonel Petrov for construction and security. They had used Yupik and Chukchi Eskimo labor. The Chukchi were native to the peninsula. The Yupiks were virtually slaves. Their antecedents had been visiting from their homelands around the Aleutians at the time of the Alaska Purchase and had been forced to stay. They had never forgotten their heritage, yearning for the east and the tribe they left behind. And now they paid the price.

One of the "Greenpeace" ships rode at anchor. Despite the general's caution about early identification, it had a huge vertical rainbow painted amidships and a white dove on both port and starboard sides of the bow, abaft the anchor ports.

The second ship, a one-hundred-eighty-foot trawler equipped with concealed missile launchers and the latest in detection electronics, all of French manufacture, had cleared the port four days earlier. It was in the Beaufort Sea, lying off the North Slope of Alaska near Prudhoe Bay and the oil fields inland from the town of Deadhorse.

Below its decks, a group of ten Yupik Eskimos, short and stocky men, trained in covert commando warfare and espionage, checked their equipment. They all carried the Finnish version of the Kalashnikov. It was lighter and more reliable than the Russian AK-47. Dressed in black wet suits against the cold of Arctic waters, they had blackened their faces for camouflage. They wore black stevedore caps and black webbing strung with grenades. Big pockets had been sewn into the fatigues worn over the wet suits to provide room for extra clips. Four of the group carried packsacks filled with plastique and electronic timers. The smell of greasepaint and blubber wafted on a slight breeze.

Josef Garin, one of the assault force, felt ill at ease about making the raid. He was short and stout like the others, but more resolute. More than most of his fellows, he had never forgotten the stories of his true homeland. He chafed to be rid of the Russian yoke, and it bothered him that his newly acquired military training could lead to a confrontation with his own kind. But he had taken the training and had excelled. He was sure the ways of war would serve him well some day.

On the Alaskan shore, the town of Deadhorse slept in the cold of a spring morning. It was small, mainly an outpost of one-story frame dwellings and metal storehouses. The residents were mostly from the southern states of America, oil people and builders of steel tanks. Some were native Inupiak Eskimo.

A mile from shore, the rainbow-painted trawler launched four rubber crafts. Garin was in the first of them. They came in with muffled outboards, the noise drowned by the sound of the surf and the howling wind.

Within minutes, the raiders stepped ashore. A cold wind pushed at their backs, the untainted air challenging the smells of the oil community. Routine took over, ingrained habits from the grueling months of training. Garin helped beach his craft and silently crept inland past the sleeping town toward the towering derricks that sucked oil from underground pools. Storage tanks stood like massive sentinels against a graying dawn sky.

He could hear the barking of dogs. That didn't bother him. Dogs had barked in northern towns for centuries: they barked at the sounds of seals cavorting and at small game that crept near the town.

Garin had been briefed well. He knew that the oil riggers and tank men would still be in soft beds, reluctant to leave the warmth of partnered flesh.

In their black garb, Garin and the others flitted from rig to rig like a stream of wraiths blown by the wind, silent and deadly. They swiftly laid charges at each of the tanks.

Their job was not to kill, but to destroy and create an illusion. The order pleased Garin. He didn't want to kill. He worked fast with the other men, his footwear of caribou hide making no noise on the tundra and hardtop roads. They ran from derrick to derrick, planting charges at their base, concentrating on towers and pump houses, making sure the charges, some phosphorus, would flame the oil when they let go.

The Yupik glanced at his watch. It seemed much less, but they had been ashore for fifteen minutes. The charges were laid. They had been timed perfectly. The first was to blow when they were almost aboard the mother ship.

As he moved with the others to the shore again, he thought the whole plan foolish. The charges would take out the Americans' valuable installations. The boat that was painted to resemble the *Rainbow Warrior* would point the finger of suspicion at the Greenpeace movement.

Could the Americans be so gullible? Could the world? He though not, but he had to follow orders. He was an Eskimo peasant in a Russian world—the lowest of the low. He knew the Yupik had been chosen so no Russians would be seen if anything went wrong, not even Chukchi Russians. Even the men aboard were all foreigners.

Halfway through the jumble of wood huts, racing for the shore, Garin heard the first storage tank blow. An uncertain dawn changed to midday as orange flames licked the sky. Thick black smoke and the smell of burning fuel followed the billowing of flame, propelled toward the huts by the blast.

"Goddamn stupid timers!" he bellowed soundlessly, the words forming only in his mind and not escaping through his lips. "Goddamn equipment never worked! Never! Despite all the stupid, useless training. Hell!" He tried to shout, tried to voice the words that wouldn't come.

The assault force raced for the beach and the boats. Tall men staggered from the huts, confused and drugged with sleep, dragging guns after them.

Panicking, the Yupiks began to fire. Garin saw his friend, Iktuk, hold his finger on the trigger of his AK and send out a steady hail of steel until the firing pin clicked on an empty chamber. He yanked out the magazine, slapped in another and continued to fire. Iktuk always used more ammunition than the others, Garin thought, but he was the best.

The men who had straggled from their beds were going down like reeds before the wind, their shredded flesh splattering on the weathered wood of the shacks.

Garin's companions pulled pins on grenades and tossed them wildly as they ran for the boats. A dozen of the big men fell, screaming. A giant of a blond man raised a shotgun and pulled the trigger. As the large-bore boomed out, the giant was cut in half by a hail of steel-jacketed slugs. Iktuk took a full charge in the face and fell back, the mass of pulp that had been his head staining the water around Garin.

More men streamed from the huts, pressing for the shore. For a few seconds the noise hurt Garin's ears. Nothing in training had prepared him for this. The Kalashnikov chattered in his hands. He reloaded and pumped steel in a steady stream at anything that moved near the huts. Most of the Americans were down, their bodies in grotesque piles. Some were slumped alone against their own front doors, their blood a part of the landscape.

Within minutes, it was over. Garin pulled Iktuk to the lead boat and dumped the limp body over the side.

ON A PROMONTORY that circled the north end of Prudhoe Bay, less than a mile from the town, an Inuit slept in a sealskin tent, as he often did to get away from the confines of Deadhorse civilization. In a rhapsody of sexual fantasy, he cavorted nude with the women from his collection of *Penthouse* magazines. He dreamed on, blissfully unaware of the silent approach of the pseudo *Rainbow Warrior*.

When the tanks exploded, Charlie Dayo flung himself from his tent, the image of dancing nudes quickly vanishing as he struggled with the noise and vibration of reality and the soft flesh of fantasy.

The name *Charlie* had been passed from one generation to the next in the Inuit family that had migrated from the Yukon more than fifty years earlier. Charlie Johnson had been a Scotsman, a trader and their friend. The current Charlie was a cousin of Chank Dayo, an ex-Marine who had died fighting the Spetsnaz with the SOBs. Charlie had the typical Eskimo build—short and stocky—and his body hairless. A loner, he was a fisherman and a hunter.

He shook his head, trying to focus, reached for his binoculars and grabbed his gun from beneath a covering of furs.

The oil tanks were a mass of flames, and a cloud of dense black smoke was drifting his way, smelling of burning oil and cordite. Most of the derricks were down. Men running from the houses were chewed up by hundreds of rounds of automatic-weapon fire. The popping noise came in waves.

His long dark hair blew in the smoke-filled wind as Charlie put his black eyes to the rubber-cushioned eyepieces. He swung his glasses to the invaders who were retreating to rubber boats waiting on shore. Even a mile away, he couldn't mistake the way they moved: they were his people.

He was too far away to take a shot, and by the time he could move close enough, they would be gone. Even as he watched, the black-clad men, all short and stocky like him, scrambled into their boats and were shoving off from shore.

He turned the glasses to the ship that poked its bow out of the gray morning light. She was big, about two hundred feet. The glow from the ruptured tanks illuminated the rainbow painted on her hull amidships. A big white dove had been painted close to her bow. Her name, in huge white letters, was easy to read.

*Rainbow Warrior.* Greenpeace!

## 3

William Starfoot II had wanted to hunt Alaska brown bear since he and Chank Dayo had talked about the majestic animals when they were sitting over camp fires between the chunks of hell they shared in Vietnam. For a full-blooded Osage who identified with the old ways, hunting Alaska brown bear was the ultimate dream. Starfoot couldn't believe he'd finally made it.

It was a cold and lonely place. Terror Bay, Kodiak Island, faced Shelikof Strait, its shores pounded by high tides blown in by fierce storms off the Gulf of Alaska. Above the bay, the mountains were covered by dense alder, and in the open, grasses grew more than six feet high.

Alex Nanos stood surveying the scene at Starfoot's side. They had seen deer, fox, otter and wild fowl in profusion, but no brown bears. They knew what they might face—huge beasts of legendary power, cunning creatures moving like ghosts through alders and brush, capable of taking four or five rounds from a high-powered rifle without slowing their charge.

Starfoot, nicknamed "Billy Two" by his friends, was built like a bear. At six feet six, with shoulders like Hercules and arms like oaks, he was a match for any animal that lived. His fellow SOB, Alex "the Greek" Nanos, was a head shorter, a body builder, as well muscled as his gargantuan buddy. Both had permits to shoot a bear, but Billy doubted that his friend, as fierce as he was in combat, would put a slug into one of the magnificent beasts when the time came. Alex was a lover, not a hunter, more like a dedicated womanizer. He wouldn't shoot the bear: he would love it.

The two warriors were on a high bluff, their glasses pressed to eyes weary from searching. The sky was blue, the whole area bathed in sunlight. Suddenly Billy nudged his friend and pointed.

"Look! A bear!" he whispered.

It was beautiful, the angle of the sun turning its brown coat to gold.

"Not exactly trophy size," Nanos said. "How big?"

"A young man. Five feet, maybe." Then, within seconds, Billy whispered urgently, "Another!" His glasses pointed to the hill below them. "To the left, about a hundred and fifty feet away."

A bear reared from a creek, a salmon in its mouth. It had to be an eight-footer. They had been told the biggest would go to ten feet.

"This one is mine, Alex. Okay?"

"Take it."

Billy unslung his rifle, checked the magazine and cranked a round into the breech as quietly as he knew how.

They were in deep grass, downwind of the beast. The range was right. The animal could be spooked any second, and the native American knew he couldn't hesitate. They had been out seven days, and these were the first bears they'd seen.

Billy stood, brought the cross hairs to focus on the animal's rib cage. The rifle roared once. The slug tore through the bear's lungs. The huge animal let out a howl. Seconds later it went down and didn't move.

Billy walked in cautiously, with Nanos bringing up the rear. The Greek had his rifle at the ready, casting his eyes from left to right for the other bear, but it had taken off.

Billy's trophy lay on gravel on the side of the creek, its blood flowing into the crystal water. It was beautiful, about six years old, maybe seven. The head was large, with a long snout. The animal's face and nose broadened into a perfect shape, and its hide looked flawless, with not a rub mark on it.

"Couldn't have been out of the den for more than a couple of weeks. A beauty," Billy said, leaning down to look into the broad brown face and the black snout.

He handed his rifle to Nanos, slipped out of his backpack and reached for his skinning knife....

"Wake up, Billy! Wake up!" Nanos's boisterous voice ended the Indian's reveries. "We're starting our descent into Deadhorse."

Billy Two shrugged off sleep and glanced around the bush plane they had hired, afraid their hunting trip had all been a dream, too.

In front of them the pilot sat at the controls, his pipe streaming smoke, as it did sixteen hours a day. Beside them, their packsacks were piled in vacant seats. It hadn't been a dream, and the memory of their week in the wilds of Terror Bay rushed back. He'd been right about Nanos. The Greek was a terror in battle, a maniac in the bedroom, but he couldn't kill a bear.

And he'd been wrong about himself. He couldn't kill a bear, either. At the last moment, sighting down the rifle scope, he'd jerked the barrel upward and fired high.

The noble beast, master of its wild domain, vanished into the thick woods beyond the creek.

He lowered the rifle and looked shamefaced at the Greek.

Nanos shrugged. "Hell. We already kill to live."

Billy Two nodded. "But not for pleasure."

"Secret?" the Greek suggested.

Starfoot had looked back in the direction of the vanished bear.

"Deal."

The Osage wiped his eyes to clear away the sleep and looked through the bush plane's window. They had left the endless forests behind, and the Beaufort Sea glimmered across the northern horizon. To the west a distant clearing on the shore marked the town of Deadhorse.

Billy Two had once been there with Claude Hayes to recruit Chank Dayo for Barrabas. It was a long time ago.

Chank had been the best damned pilot in these parts. He had flown them out of a hellhole in the Siberian gulags, and he'd bought it when the Russian GRU's elite Spetsnaz corps had come after them and demolished Lee Hatton's villa in Majorca.

Claude Hayes, a former Navy frogman and an African freedom fighter, had hated Deadhorse. It had been winter, closed in, cold as an old whore's heart.

"Don't worry, Alex," Billy teased. "Even Claude raved about the woman I got for him. You'll see."

Satisfied, Nanos settled back until the plane banked to port. "What the hell's been going on down there?" he asked suddenly, looking out his window as they circled to land.

The oil derricks were mostly crumpled piles of steel. Frame houses were piles of charcoal. Most of the storage tanks looked like charred holes in the ground. It looked as though a tornado had swept through the town.

Charlie Dayo was waiting for them on the tarmac. A short man like his cousin Chank, he was sturdy and smooth-faced. His long black hair stuck out from a wool toque. He wore a lightweight jacket and parka, jeans and Kodiak hiking boots.

"Billy, Billy Two," he shouted. "You big bastard. How the hell are you?"

The SOBs towered over the smaller man. Billy picked him up and swung him around. "I'm great. How else would a man feel in God's country?" He immediately told his old friend about the big one that got away.

"Good. Better that than a trophy for a boardroom huckster."

"Charlie. Meet my best buddy." The Osage introduced Alex Nanos.

"I knew Chank. We had a special friendship," Nanos said.

"You are welcome here," Charlie said with feeling. "Let's get over to my shack. Got a case of Johnny Walker not even opened. What do you say?"

"What the hell's been happening here?" Billy asked as they walked to the hut.

"Very weird, Billy. I saw some of it. Tell you all about it. Let's get a glass in our hands."

They walked the two hundred yards past burned-out buildings to Charlie's shack. People scurried like ants, carrying lumber, window casements, doors. The sound of hammers drowned out the barking of dogs and the low howl of wind off the Beaufort Sea. The place smelled more like a lumberyard than a fishing port and oil field.

Inside, Charlie tossed a match onto kindling in a stone fireplace and waved them to hand-hewn wooden chairs. The shack was rugged, built of foot-thick logs, the chinks filled with mortar. It had two rooms, one large and functional, the other a bedroom.

The fire began to roar, and flames painted patterns of light on the rough walls. Charlie ripped open the top of a cardboard box, pulled out a bottle of Johnny Walker Red, unscrewed the cap, then handed out chipped white mugs.

"I got no mix."

"This will do, Charlie," Billy said.

Nanos held out his mug.

"Must look bad to you out there. Sleepy little oil town when you were here, eh?" Charlie said, filling his mug to the brim.

"Can't believe it," Billy said. "Looks more like a battleground."

"That's what it was. No radio where you was. Surprised your pilot didn't say."

"The man answers questions, and he flies. When you don't talk, he don't talk," Nanos offered. "Hell of a pilot, though."

"Queerest thing I ever seen," Charlie began. He told them about his sleeping out on the point sometimes, just to get the hell away from people, and what he'd seen that morning. "I told the state police. I told the FBI. And I told some other guys with the button-down collars—could have been CIA or something." He took a good slug of the Scotch. "Hell, I'm tired of telling."

"They stick around long?" Nanos asked.

"A couple days. Smart bastards figured they knew it all."

"Tell 'em everything, Charlie?" Billy asked.

Charlie Dayo looked at his big friend and grinned. "The guys in the boats were Eskimo. I didn't tell them that."

"Who were they?"

"Damned if I know. I was too far off. They weren't from around here."

"But the boat was definitely Greenpeace?" Nanos asked.

"How the hell do I know? I saw the plumage. It was like the boat we had in here a couple of years ago, but I didn't take pictures, you know?"

"Many killed?" Billy asked.

"Brutal. Maybe thirty. I think it was thirty-one. All but one were from the lower states, oilmen, tank men. One of ours was up early and got in the way. No kids or women."

"Something else?" Billy asked, knowing from his friend's expression that he was sorely puzzled by the raid.

"I don't think they expected to kill anyone." He downed the last of the drink and looked from one to the other. "Something else I didn't tell the cops. They used AKs."

"How'd you know that?" Nanos asked.

Charlie picked up the bottle and filled all three mugs.

"Hey, I was a dog soldier in Nam, okay?" he said. "I know a Kalashnikov when I hear one."

"Why didn't the cops find AK cartridges? Some slugs from the huts?"

"All the cartridges were in the water. Probably swept away."

"What about the slugs in the huts...in the bodies?" Charlie asked.

"Could have found some. They didn't say."

"Anything else, Charlie? Anything at all?" Nanos asked.

"One last thing. It's so crazy I didn't tell anyone." He took a slug of the Scotch and looked at the two men sitting around his table. "The ship flew a tricolor. Now, why the hell would it fly a flag at all? Let alone a French flag?"

"Sounds crazy. I agree," Nanos said. "First of all, Greenpeace wouldn't do anything to destroy the ecology. They're pacifist, for chrissakes. Second, why would anyone want to advertise their nationality? Crazy."

Billy looked at Alex, and a signal passed between them. Barrabas should know about this.

"How'd an Eskimo get a name like Charlie?" Nanos asked, changing the subject.

Charlie grinned. "An honor for me from my tribe. This is Inupik country. My people came here maybe sixty, seventy years ago from the Yukon." He took a gulp from the mug, reached for a pack of stogies and offered them around. Nanos took one.

"Charlie Johnson was our friend in the Canadian government's Department of Native Affairs or something. A good man. Anyway, one Dayo male from each generation is named Charlie in his honor. And how you been, Billy? I heard some Russkies got into your head real bad."

"It gets better, Charlie. It gets better," Billy said, suddenly uncomfortable. Although he felt better than he had for a long time, even vague reminders of his painful experience made him feel as though someone was walking over his grave. "Whatever happened to Noweena? Did she stick around when Chank didn't come back?"

"Who was Noweena?" Nanos asked.

Billy winked at Charlie. The game was on. Noweena had been a brown bear, Chank's pet. Last time Billy was there, they had conned Hayes into believing the old tale about a guest's sleeping with the Eskimo host's wife.

Hayes had been reluctant to insult his host, and Chank had retired from the scene with dignity.

Billy had pushed Hayes in with Noweena, but the joke had backfired. The huge brute had gone after both SOBs, chasing them onto a roof. She almost had them for dinner.

"Noweena was Chank's wife," Charlie fibbed. "Left town. Used to ask after Claude a lot. She really enjoyed him."

"Enjoyed? What the hell does that mean?" Nanos asked.

"Best lay she ever had, except for Chank. That's what she said." Charlie kept a straight face, the expression he used over poker games with the oilmen.

"Chank's wife?" Nanos asked.

Billy put down his drink. "Mind if Alex and I have a little talk?" he asked Charlie. "In the bedroom?"

"Help yourself," Charlie said, starting to slur from the contents of his seldom empty mug.

Billy took Nanos by the arm, led him to the bedroom and closed the door. The room was small, almost filled by a huge double bed made of logs. One small dresser stood in a corner with a pitcher of water and a basin on top.

Billy Two spoke urgently. "I can't sleep with her. I was with her last time."

"Who? Sleep with who?" Nanos's eyes grew wide with temptation.

"Kaweetha, Charlie's wife. It's the custom here. For a guest to sleep with his host's wife!"

"*Wife?* I ain't sleeping with no friend's wife. Not with him knowing, I ain't." Nanos got up and paced the room. "Shit, man! Got to be someone else here, right?"

"You got to, Alex. It's an insult if you don't. The woman can't hold up her head with the other women. She'll think she's ugly or something."

"She probably is."

"Kaweetha? No way. She's . . . she's awesome."

"I don't believe this. Where the hell is she now? Why wasn't she here cooking or something?"

"The other women are getting her ready. Something like a bridal ritual. She'll be here soon."

"Getting her ready?"

"Bathing, oiling, that sort of thing. Look, they've been doing this for centuries. You can't come in here and insult them."

Billy watched Alex closely. He knew his man well. The Greek had not only swallowed it, he was starting to preen.

"Charlie and I are going to leave. Use the water and the cloths here and clean yourself up a little. She'll come to you alone."

"If you say so," Alex said, then stood, pensive. "How long will she stay? You know?"

"All night, Alex. All-l-l night long."

Billy closed the door after him and motioned Charlie out of the shack. They walked three blocks to the hotel, the largest building still standing in town. Behind the desk, the biggest woman Billy had ever seen was holding forth with a group of locals. Her voice filled the lobby, its volume at a decibel that was close to the pain threshold.

"Kaweetha?" Billy asked Charlie, and broke out laughing.

"Used to be the town whore, then a madame down in Fairbanks. Came back and built the hotel."

The two pranksters approached as the group was breaking up. Kaweetha looked at Billy and grinned, her mouth a flash of gold. Up close, he could see she wasn't just fat. She was solid, weighing in at more than three hundred pounds, and powerful. He wondered if he could take her in a fair fight: she looked that strong.

They told her about the joke. After a hearty laugh, she spread her arms and declared, "Let's go."

They walked to the street. Charlie looked like a midget beside the other two. A crowd gathered and followed, obviously in a carnival mood.

At Charlie's shack, Kaweetha turned to them and waved, then silently opened the door.

Nanos came out of the bedroom, naked.

*"Hello, honey,"* she said, the force of her voice enough to bend a small tree. *"I hope you're half the man my Charlie is."*

She picked up the stunned Nanos, kicking the door to the bedroom closed with one foot.

Through walls a foot thick, they heard Nanos's screams.

*"I'll get you for this, Billy. You son of a bitch!"*

A struggle shook the house for a second or two, then there were some spine-tingling shouts, followed by silence.

THE NEXT MORNING in a boat at anchor ten miles west of Deadhorse, Billy Two and Nanos floated on a smooth sea, their lines dangling in the water. The sun shone brightly off the silver offshore chop. Wild birds and waterfowl streaked overhead.

It had taken them more than an hour to find the spot Charlie had recommended for Arctic char.

Billy kept glancing at his friend. The Greek hadn't said a word for an hour. He hadn't said much of anything since Billy had roused him from a pile of furs on

Charlie's bed. Kaweetha had left at about four in the morning.

Alex seemed to be dazed, and he didn't have any energy. It was as if a sheet of plastic had been drawn between him and the rest of the world.

Occasionally the Greek would mutter something that sounded like "Hot damn!" But it didn't sound as though he was mad at anyone.

Billy wondered if he was trying to express an opinion on something. The only time he'd seen Nanos like this had been at a beauty contest in Florida where Alex had scored with every contestant. His state had been similar, but not quite as severe. That time, it had taken him three days to lose the glazed look.

Well, they were in no hurry. Billy had left a message for Barrabas at the Caribbean island where he was vacationing, asking him to call back at three, Alaska time.

"You all right, Alex?" the oversize Indian asked.

"She . . . hell, she . . . I never seen anything like it." He shook his head in disbelief. "Hot damn!"

"Good or bad?"

"Different. Big. Powerful. Best fuckin' woman I ever met . . . in her own way . . . best . . ."

And that was all Billy got out of him for the next two days.

**4**

The spring air in Washington had warmed far beyond that of the forty-ninth state. The capital's famous cherry blossoms had filled the air with their heady fragrance a month earlier. Now the city smelled of fresh-turned sod and new plantings. Even the pollution from the constant traffic around Capitol Hill was unable to overcome it.

Walker Jessup grasped the doorframe of his stretch limo and pulled his three hundred pounds into the morning sunlight. Though the heat of summer had not yet hit the capital, his suit was damp with sweat. Jessup was seldom free from sweat since he'd put on the lard and changed his action from CIA fieldwork to brokering independent projects.

They called him "the Fixer."

Jessup took an elevator at the back of the building, preferring to remain out of sight as much as possible, particularly when visiting the man who was his conduit to a mysterious committee of legislators who authorized much of his work.

On the top floor of the senatorial office block, Jessup opened a door without knocking. One woman occupied the outer office, the senator's dragon lady, Miss Roseline.

"He called me," Jessup said.

The woman sat behind a computer console at an antique desk. Slim, big-busted, she seemed to demand attention but had a daunting air of indifference about her. She looked up and waved him in.

Jessup walked ponderously across the rich carpet, opened and closed a door, shutting out the console noise. The inner office was large, furnished with oversize, ornately carved furniture. Tapestries hung from the walls, sharing the space with oil paintings. Not exactly what the average U.S. senator would choose. In the midst of all the splendor, the senator looked like a shrunken gnome.

"Come in, Jessup." He indicated a seat at one side of his huge desk. Since the senator's run-in with a cult leader in Honduras, he had been confined to a wheelchair, his legs useless. He had become more and more bitter, harder than ever to deal with. His infirmities seemed to fuel his hunger for power.

Jessup had seen a great change in the man since they had met to form the Barrabas team. The senator was a short man, but he had been an immaculate dresser, and his presence had seemed to add to his stature. Now he shrank into the wheelchair, his clothes ill-fitting, and his temper worse than ever. His scalp was glossy, closer to his skull. He looked like a cadaver on wheels.

"This one is really different," the senator began.

"How different? Are we talking about Alaska?"

"One of our fifty states, if you remember. We're talking about U.S. of A. soil."

"And you want some of my people to handle it." Jessup paused and let his gaze rove thoughtfully over the room, examining the tapestries glinting with gold thread. Then he looked the senator in the eye and continued. "They handled the Florida problem. The governor down there was real pleased. But I'd have thought a show of force like we did with Libya would be better for Alaska."

"Don't ever think of entering politics, Jessup. You don't try to flex your muscles with the big bear. Can't you just see two battle fleets steaming through the Bering Strait and forming up around the Chukchi Peninsula? That would be madness. The Florida thing was a terrorist threat. This could be the first Russian crack at one of our states."

"I heard the boat was Greenpeace."

"A ruse, and not a very good one. I've talked to Steve Smith, an American director of Greenpeace. Their new *Rainbow Warrior* is off the coast of England, protesting the dumping of atomic waste at sea."

The senator wheeled out from behind his desk. He rolled beside Jessup and set the brake on his chair. "I know the guy. He wouldn't lie. Besides, the ship couldn't have attacked in Alaska and crossed to Europe in time."

"So it has to be the Russians?"

"The way I figure it, someone wants to discredit Greenpeace and get at us at the same time."

"What about the French?" Jessup asked. "They sent the original *Rainbow Warrior* to the bottom in Auckland harbor."

"Maybe. But they wouldn't attack Alaska. Typical Russian stuff. They know the ruse is thin, but it doesn't matter to them. Get in and do the damage. Let the bleeding hearts scream. More their style."

"They hate Greenpeace that much?"

"I'm not going to catalog their relationship for you, Jessup. Suffice to say Greenpeace has been under Russian skin for a long time. The only organization on earth to get away with it. Up to now."

The senator had moved his chair around the desk so he would be close to Jessup, and now Miss Roseline entered carrying a tray. She poured for them both and turned away. As she left, Jessup had to admit she had some attractive assets. Too bad she sat on them most of the time.

"We got more trouble than that," the senator said, picking up his cup. "This is ripe for the CIA and the FBI. The military feels it's their baby. They've all had people up there snooping around. The President has called them all off. Capitol Hill is hot. A lot of noses out of joint around this town today."

"So it's your baby now?"

"*Our* baby."

Up close, the senator looked worse than ever. Jessup wondered if he was a sick man. "Need lots of scope on this one. And lots of backup," he said.

"Explain."

"Alaska is one hell of a big place. Sure, they hit at the extreme north first, but we're vulnerable all along the coast, and that's one hell of a coastline."

"Are you saying your Barrabas people can't handle it?"

"No. But we'll need both sea and air transport, and the best you've got. We'll need all your clout. And I'll have to get closer to the action."

"Explain." The senator was no fool, but he insisted that everything be spelled out.

"We'll need a Coast Guard cutter, an Air Force reconnaissance plane, a jet chopper and maybe some satellite surveillance."

"What? You've got only eight people, for chrissakes. Do they each get a few million dollars' worth of equipment to play with?"

"They won't need it all at once. And they can handle it."

"Jesus! If I didn't have to deal with . . ." The senator let the sentence trail off, leaving the thought unspoken. Jessup knew his problem. It was pride. He had to get the job done, but he hated to be compromised. He needed Jessup, and he didn't like having to show his weakness.

"I'm going to take it easy on you this time, Senator. Five hundred thousand apiece. And we'll try not to foul up too much of your valuable equipment."

"Get the hell out of here, Jessup. Round up your people and give me a list of what you need. Whatever they use, we're going to paint out official markings. They go in as private citizens, as usual.''

Jessup was halfway to the door. "So what else is new?" He closed the door behind him.

AT THE TOP of the Caribbean island, Nile Barrabas lay on his stomach on a fiber mat, soaking up the sun, with a woman beside him. She was on her back, and the small black plastic shields protecting her eyes from the tropic sun were her only covering. He'd met her in Washington. She was a very complete woman, the perfect companion on an almost deserted isle: she talked little, but when she did, she usually had something interesting to say. Otherwise, she took the sun and physical contact regularly.

They were head-to-toe. Barrabas faced north. Beyond the cone-shaped Petit St. Vincent where they lay, he could see the string of islands framed in azure blue, and in the distance, Bequia and St. Vincent. A speck rose from the farthest island, an aircraft taking off from the nearest airport. Had his companion been looking, she would have seen a similar string of islands to the south, anchored by Grenada, the last and largest of the chain.

Their forty-acre island was a paradise. Connected by winding paths, eight thatched cottages, all different colors, perched on the hillside. A central building housed the owner, an intimate bar and a gourmet dining room. A hundred feet below the patio bar, three cruising sailboats bobbed in the light chop: a forty-foot Morgan, a leased CSY44 and a fifty-foot trimaran. Sailors were always welcomed by the seafaring owner of the island. It was a luxury stop in the center of the Grenadines. Sea smells, mixed with the exotic aroma from neighboring cane plantations, wafted in on constant southwesterlies.

During the short holiday the woman had turned a dark coffee color all over. Barrabas had enjoyed the rest, the frolicking in the surf and in their bed. But it was beginning to pall. His finely tuned mind and body were crying out for a challenge.

He shaded his eyes and looked down the hill at the central building. Two signal flags flew below the owner's pennant. The white flag announced the happy hour, and the green flag told the occupants of cottage green that they had a message. Barrabas's cottage was green.

He raised himself on one elbow and looked at the woman. She was rock-still, dozing in the afternoon sun, beautiful and vulnerable, her long legs and torso demarcated by a tuft of black hair that matched her long tresses. He felt a mixture of sadness and relief: it was over. The message would be a recall. It couldn't be anything else.

Barrabas rolled on his back, reached for a pair of sun-bleached shorts and pulled them on. He stood, his six-foot four-inch frame towering over the woman. The breeze tugged at his short white hair, a souvenir of his Vietnam years and a bullet crease across one temple.

"We've got a message," he said. "I'm going down. Meet you back at our place."

At the patio bar he picked up an extension. "Harry, it's Nile."

"I got a number from the mainland," the owner said. "Just a minute. Got it right here somewhere."

Barrabas waited, hearing the rustling of papers. Harry was a great guy, he thought idly, but disorganized.

"Here it is. The man said it was urgent." Harry carefully read off the number.

The nine-one-seven area code was unfamiliar.

"Connect me, Harry," Barrabas commanded.

In the two minutes it took, Barrabas watched the trimaran hoist anchor and take off under full sail, then Alex Nanos came on the line.

"You get any bears?" Barrabas asked, surprised by the familiar voice. He wondered what in hell Alex would call about. Between jobs, he was usually preoccupied with chasing and bedding beautiful women.

"Uh, well, someday I'll tell you about the one that got away. We're up here with Chank's people. You heard the news down there?"

"What news?" He picked a complimentary stogie from a box on the bar and lit up. The bartender placed a frosted glass of Dutch gin beside his hand.

"A ship pulled in here about a week ago, dropped off a landing party at dawn. Destroyed oil derricks. Blew most of the storage tanks."

"Any clues who did it?"

"The ship had Greenpeace markings. You know— the rainbow colors and the white doves."

"Didn't the French sink their ship?"

"They bought a new one."

"Hell, Alex. It couldn't be them. Oil spills ruin the ecology."

"The place was crawling with CIA, FBI and state police before we arrived."

"So why call me? If Jessup wants us, he knows where I am."

"A cousin of Chank's is here, name of Charlie Dayo. Turns out he was the best witness. He told us some stuff he didn't tell the police. Thought you might pass it on to Jessup."

Barrabas sipped on the Jenever gin he'd learned to drink in Amsterdam. "What did he tell you?"

"Three things. The raiders were all Eskimos. He wasn't close enough to guess which tribe they might be from. Second, they used AKs."

"The weapons don't mean anything. But only three countries—besides Greenland—have Eskimo populations, and one is Russia."

"That's what we thought, Colonel."

"What's the third thing?"

"The old trawler flew the French flag."

Barrabas thought for a few seconds. "The French have been charged formally with blowing up the Greenpeace ship in Auckland harbor," he said. "But they wouldn't be stupid enough to try to...and they wouldn't fly their own flag."

"That's what we thought, Colonel."

"You got any weapons there, Alex?"

"Just a couple of hunting rifles. Why?"

Barrabas's mind had been racing while they talked. He knew Chank's hometown well. It was the northern terminal of the Alaska pipeline. "They could come back, Alex. The pipeline terminal's still intact, right?"

"Shit. We didn't think of that. Strange, but the police and the spooks already pulled out, though gradually. No military here at all."

"Maybe Jessup's into it already. Get your hands on some real weapons and wait for me to call," Barrabas said, blowing smoke into the warm breeze on the patio. "Something smells here, Alex. Could be our people don't want a show of military. If the Soviets are behind it, we could start a real shooting war."

JESSUP HAD JUST RETURNED HOME when the telephone rang. He'd had time to pull off his coat and head for the refrigerator. He sat at the kitchen table with a cold Coors in one hand and a mammoth submarine sandwich in the other. Jessup had them made specially for him at a delicatessen down the street from his apartment, and kept a half dozen on hand for snacking.

"Jessup," he snapped, his mouth half-full.

"Barrabas. I just heard about the Alaska raid."

"You still in the Caribbean?"

"Yup. Nanos called a few minutes ago."

"Nanos?"

"By coincidence he and Billy are in Alaska on a bear hunt. Chank Dayo's people live at Deadhorse, the site of the raid. Alex and Billy are there right now."

"Tell them to stay there. How fast can you get to Washington?"

"Tomorrow. About dinnertime."

Jessup thought about the time frame and the information they'd have to exchange. His favorite restaurant would be as good a place as any.

"Meet me at Le Gourmet. I'll be there from seven to ten."

THE TALL MAN SAT in a black leather swivel chair in the Oval Office, his feet propped up on the desk. He was dressed casually, his white T-shirt showing under a disreputable cardigan.

It was his favorite time of the day. At times he would share it with his wife in their quarters, away from his demanding staff, and review their day. But she was away in Michigan on one of her many public appearances, so he was alone with his thoughts.

Those thoughts would weigh heavily on the average man. But he had a greater than average capacity for reponsibility. He was preoccupied with current problems, some of which filled the pages of daily journals around the country. The summit was still a hot item. A team negotiating nuclear arms was still in Vienna.

The Russians had just arrested an American journalist on trumped-up charges, hoping that they could trade the poor slob for one of theirs, a man who had spied on America for years.

The famous profile tightened into rock-hardness, and the tall man swore under his breath.

He was a fighter. His method of handling the Russians was hard talk and tough negotiating. He wouldn't hesitate for a minute if they ever stepped out of line where he could nail them. He knew one of their weaknesses better than they knew it themselves. As with the Arabs and the Chinese, their weakness was a concern with "face." It appeared as though they would commit any act, any international takeover with impunity, but their image in the international press worried them. They had a dread of looking foolish.

He was determined that sometime during his tenure, he would hold them up to the international press and show the world just what they were.

A pot of coffee was kept hot for him in an alcove on the far wall, close to the huge glass table where he conducted most of his business during the day. The aroma floated over to him. He uncurled his six-foot-four height and ambled over.

He had just brought a steaming brew to his lips when a faint buzz sounded near his desk.

He frowned heavily. Only a handful of people knew the number—he knew what the sound meant.

Taking the coffee with him, he folded his long, slim frame into the chair again. Opening a drawer in the desk, he took a black receiver from an ornate box concealed beneath several files.

"Yes" was all he said.

"When you asked me to handle a few jobs for you, you said to keep you clear of it," the senator said.

"I take it you want me to get involved in something personally."

"I can handle the director of Central Intelligence, and maybe the director of the Federal Bureau. But I don't have all the leverage I'd need with members of your cabinet."

"Sounds serious."

"Our own soil. You've heard about the Alaska raid."

"I'm not getting involved. Political suicide. I told you that at the time of the Florida raids."

"This is different, sir. It's the Russians. I've put Jessup and his people to work again, but they need a lot more hardware, and a lot more pull. Your Secretary of Defense has to be involved."

"No way!"

"We can't let the Soviets get away with this."

"Are you sure it's them?" The tall man stood and paced around the desk, unwinding the long telephone cord. He stared intently at the carpet. "They'd be fools to get involved in the Alaska thing."

"They've been known to make mistakes, sir." The senator waited expectantly, squirming in his wheelchair impatiently. A surge of excitement coursed through his withered body.

"What do you see? Give me the worst scenario and the best."

"The best? Barrabas and his people using some heavy-duty hardware supplied by our military and destroying all attackers who try to get at our Alaska oil." He hesitated a few seconds before going on. "The worst? The Russian set up a squadron of fighters and a few missile-carrying ships to destroy our mercenaries."

"The main thing," the tall man said, then paused significantly. "Our objective has to be proof of Russian complicity. Absolute proof."

"Suppose it's within our grasp, but the Russians block us with military power?"

"If it's on American soil or in American waters, our military will appear as if by magic."

The senator sat at his desk for a minute, digesting the words. He hadn't really expected The Man to go that far.

"We've got to get them with their pants down. If you can, I'm with you all the way." The tall man leaned back in his chair with an air of finality. "But keep me out of it if you can."

"If we can. By God, if we can catch them with their hands in the cookie jar," the senator said.

"I didn't know you were a religious man, Senator," the man in the Oval Office chuckled as he replaced the receiver.

He mulled over the situation in Alaska. He was familiar with the near-miracles Barrabas and his people had accomplished in the past. He realized that the best results had been achieved when the mercs were in total control. No one was more aware of the problems with interservice rivalries. Barrabas could get caught in the middle, separated from the chief executive by a wall of red tape.

Thoughts swirled around in his tired brain. The Russians attacking Alaska. Maybe this was it—the big white light that was going to show the world what phonies the Russians were.

He'd do anything to get at the truth. Anything!

Then he followed up his own thoughts. He foresaw squadrons of Russian fighters facing his Alaska forces, and ships carrying missiles in a deadly face-off.

Jesus! He was going to have nightmares tonight.

5

A loon called from overhead as it flew down the length of the Canadian lake north of Montreal. The blanket of green leaves, newly born in that week, was in stark contrast to the dark evergreens surrounding the shore. The fresh breeze was free from the pollutants of man.

Geoff Bishop and Lee Hatton stood at the rail of the deck that almost surrounded the main building, his arm around her shoulder. They were at ease with each other, an ease that had grown strong with time. Here, away from the pressures of battle, they were lovers and confidants. In battle, working with the Soldiers of Barrabas, they were dedicated and detached.

"I can never get enough of this place," Lee said softly.

"And I can never get enough of you. Remember the first time?"

"Not likely to forget. Just before we went into Cambodia to take care of General Kon."

"We were worried the others would suspect." He moved behind her, circled her with his arms. "Not much doubt they know now."

"It really bothered me when Alex made a fool of himself over us."

"Can't say I blame him. Alex is the woman chaser. Guess he thought if anyone in the group—you know—that it should be him."

Lee laughed. "You're a prude at times, you now? 'Got me in the sack' is what you wanted to say. So say it."

"I didn't want to think about it."

Geoff Bishop looked out over his lake and thought about them and the SOBs. A Canadian, he had flown with the Royal Canadian Air Force, had been on exchange programs with the Americans at Denver's Strategic Air Command and with NATO forces in Germany. He'd flown with Canadian peacekeeping forces in Egypt and later in Cyprus. Over the years, he'd been at the controls of almost every kind of flying object the Western nations had produced.

Unwillingly he thought about another woman in his life. He'd been married while moving around the world. She hated it. He left the military at her insistence. She wanted comfort and condos, and when he produced them she still wasn't satisfied.

He also remembered the worst part of his life. Shortly after his wife left, he had flown for Canada's national airline. He had brought an L1011 down on the Trans-Canada Highway when it ran out of fuel after a foul-up in Vancouver. He was the scapegoat, despite the successful emergency landing. Fortunately, Barrabas had been on hand to fill the void with work and money.

On the SOBs' Florida mission Geoff had saved the state governor from a terrorist bomb, disappearing in the subsequent explosion. No body had been found, and he was taken for dead. Press journalists who were present mistook him for the terrorist he had stopped.

Geoff Bishop became a wanted man, his face plastered across the FBI bulletins while he rotted in a Beirut dungeon, the prisoner of Shiite terrorists. It was the worst of times, and only recently had it ended. Reunited at last with Lee Hatton and the SOBs, Bishop had been ordered by Walker Jessup to hide out at his mountain chalet while the FBI list was taken care of through secret channels.

He wore thick horn-rimmed glasses, and his dark curly hair had been straightened, cut short and bleached blond. He traveled with a false passport.

"I'm still a wanted man," he said, holding Lee tightly.

The woman warrior turned to nestle her face against his chest.

"Mmm," she sighed. "Wanted by me." She looked up at him, wriggling her eyebrows like a temptress. "Outlaws of desire."

Bishop laughed. After his months in solitary confinement, he'd had to learn how to laugh all over again. Lee was a good teacher.

Now he stood on the deck of his chalet in the lake country of Quebec, north of Montreal, his beautiful woman in his arms. He loved the feel of her, the slender but solid body, the dark hair and eyes. She was the most beautiful woman he'd ever known, and the smartest. He never ceased to be amazed by the way she could be soft and loving, yet in battle one of the most capable fighting machines he had ever met. Of all the SOBs, she was actually the best in hand-to-hand combat. Brought onto the team initially because they needed a doctor, she proved herself over and over.

He was brought out of his reverie by the ringing of the telephone.

"Nile?" Lee cast her eyes at him with a look of alarm.

"Not many people know my number. Let alone that I'm still alive."

He padded barefoot from the deck to the one-room interior of the log chalet. The telephone hung on an upright beam between the kitchen alcove and the stone fireplace.

"Yes?" he answered, careful not to use his name on the party line.

"It's Nile. Looks like we've got a job. Have you had the radio on?"

"The Alaska raid?"

"Yup. Lee with you?"

"Not far from here."

"Use the passport Jessup gave you. Take a plane for Fairbanks. Stay at the Alaska Inn. Billy and Alex are in a town called Deadhorse where the raid took place."

"Already?"

"They were hunting in Alaska."

"When will you be there?" Bishop asked.

"I haven't seen Jessup yet, but I know they'll want us for this job. I'm still in the Caribbean waiting for a charter plane to pick me up. I'll try to get through to Hayes and Beck from here."

Bishop's mind had been racing since the mention of Alaska. "A big place, Colonel. Maybe I should have a chopper to act as your eyes. Think Jessup has that kind of clout?"

"We're going to find out. See you in Fairbanks."

Bishop replaced the telephone and turned to look at Lee, who waited quietly nearby. He nodded. They both knew what it meant.

"Alaska" was all he had to say.

Lee came closer, a little smile playing on her lips to hide the sudden apprehension. She brushed her fingers lightly through her lover's hair.

"You have dark roots, Mr. Most-Wanted," she murmured, half-laughing. "Time for the peroxide. They're never going to take you away from me. Ever again."

THE SENATOR'S INTERCOM BUZZED. Miss Roseline's sultry voice broke through the dusty silence.

"Senator, we had a call from Jake, the elevator operator. He says Chester Good is heading our way."

"What the hell? The DCI here?"

"What do you want me to do?"

The senator thought for a moment. "It's okay. Just pass him through."

The senator had no love for the director of Central Intelligence, and the feeling was mutual. That he was on his way in, unannounced, was significant. For years, Chester Good had been trying to prove that the senator was behind a covert group operating outside the official intelligence community. He'd had no success, because, despite all his resources, he could never get a handle on them.

The door virtually flew open as the big man entered, his florid face creased by a scowl that looked incongruous with wispy hair standing on end. He was almost as fat as Jessup, with a nose that sat in the middle of his face like a withered strawberry and a mouth that was overgenerous. He was dressed in a thousand-dollar suit that looked like a sack on him.

The senator decided to play nice-guy. "Chester! Good of you to come. To what do I owe the honor?"

"You son of a bitch! You've gone behind my back again. The President has ordered me to brief you on the Alaska raid." He threw himself into a chair across from the little man and glowered, thrusting his face halfway across the desk.

"That was kind of him. What do you know about the Alaska raid?" The senator smiled, using muscles in his face that were seldom brought into play.

"Not that damned easy. Why the hell would you want to know? Why would the President order me?"

"Didn't you ask him?"

"You know damned well I didn't. I'm asking you." The big man, his multiple chins quivering with rage, edged his nose even closer, the desk pressing against his huge midsection.

"I'm on several committees involved with defense and internal security." The senator kept his face straight, though he was busting to laugh in the DCI's face. "So what are you going to tell me?" he asked.

Chester Good sat back, his lungs expelling enough air to fill a cluster of balloons. "You're up to something again. You're operating covertly behind my back, aren't you?"

The senator held out a box of cigars, knowing the DCI wouldn't refuse. Miss Roseline entered with a tray of coffee. She took her time pouring, keeping her ample bosom and deep cleavage inches from the DCI's face.

The senator wheeled from behind his desk and braked his chair across from the DCI.

When the cigar was going well and he had a cup of coffee in hand, the DCI's florid face turned from red to pink, and his heartbeat slowed to normal. But he hadn't given up the fight.

"Senator, I'm going to nail your hide to the wall one day, and that will be the happiest day of my life." He glowered until the veins in his neck stood out. "What makes you think you can get away with this, you insignificant little prick?" He blew a stream of smoke in the senator's face.

The senator's good-guy image melted away. The smile disappeared from his face. His eyes took on the appearance of a hooded viper's, cold and hard, and the upper half of his body seemed poised to strike. The skin of his emaciated skull seemed to tighten until his pate shone.

"Power," he said.

"Shit! Don't bull me, you shriveled little asshole."

"I've got a mandate from the voters for the next five years. I've got a dozen of our most powerful senators in my pocket. I sit on the most influential committees. And I've got the President's ear night and day. Now let's examine your strength."

The senator drained his cup and put it down, never taking his eyes from the fat man.

"You were handed your job by the last administration. Your influence is with the minority party. The President doesn't like you. No one on the Hill likes you. You're doing a lousy job and hanging on by your fingernails. So don't come in here raising your voice to me, *ever again*. Clear?"

Chester Good looked over his cup and swallowed. "No need to get worked up, Senator," he said in a diminutive voice.

"Now, what have your people turned up?"

"We've talked with Greenpeace, and they're in the clear. Their new ship is off the coast of England and couldn't have been off the coast of Alaska last week."

"I know that much. What else?"

"Greenpeace is not at peace internally. Several factions would like more militarism."

"And? Have they had any internal splits? Have any of their people taken off?" The senator filled his cup from the carafe, then raised it to his lips and held it poised there, prompting a fast answer.

"We've got one of their splinter group people at Langley. Been sweating him."

"And are the French or Russians behind it?" the senator asked, his face devoid of expression.

Chester Good bristled, but he went on. "Our interrogation turned up a few names—people who would give Greenpeace a hard time for money. The man we're holding thinks someone's taken money from the French. I'm not convinced. The French haven't the guts to pull a raid on us. They don't have the motivation."

"So it's the Russians," the senator said. "They can't think they're fooling anyone."

"Not their style, anyway. All they need is a ruse—a thin veneer." Now that he had calmed down, Chester Good spoke with less reservation. "The first raid might fool some people, but not a second."

"Think there'll be a second?"

Good put down his cup, flicked the ash from his cigar. "Maybe."

"You don't think they're afraid of a confrontation with us?"

"They know we won't start a war. We'll take countermeasures, save face, maybe even retaliate." He looked the senator in the eye. "Like the raid on their gulags in Siberia. You have anything to do with that?"

The senator ignored the remark. "What else can you tell me?"

"I'm going to be right on top of this. I'll have our spy satellites concentrate on that area. Maybe we can come up with something. If I see an operation in progress to counter the Russians, maybe I'll find out who's running it."

Finished, he rose ponderously from the chair and shook a finger at the wizened man in the wheelchair.

"You made it clear how you feel about me—how I'm in a bad position in this administration." His face assumed a grim look of determination. You ever hear of the good work John Edgar Hoover did to keep the Kennedys in line? Well, I've taken a leaf out of his book, and I'm getting quite good at it. So don't threaten me, Senator. And don't let me find you messing in my preserves again. I warn you."

"Sit," the senator said, the hooded look back in his eyes.

"What?"

"I said *sit*, you stupid fat bastard." The senator didn't move or gesture. He just spit out the words like missiles.

"You weren't listening very well the first time, so I'll spell it out so any oaf can understand. You are still the director of the most powerful intelligence community in the Western world because we know what to expect from you. That's the *only* reason you are still at

Langley. So listen and don't interrupt. I want all satellite intelligence on this Alaska problem routed
through me. I don't want you to interfere in any way
with countermeasures taken by this administration.
And last, I want the telephone number for your
specialists who clean up after 'wet affairs.' They could
be getting calls from Alaska.

"Now, if that's clear, I can tell you that your job
will be safe for the present. Cross me, and you'll end
up teaching freshmen in a back-country college a
thousand miles from Washington. And finally if you
try the old Hoover approach, you'll have the whole of
Washington on your back."

The senator smiled, his mouth a cruel crease in a
cadaverous face. "If you managed to understand all
that, you can get the hell out of here."

CLAUDE HAYES WOKE with a hangover, not exactly
sure where he was. His face was resting on flesh, soft
and warm. He turned his head. Two rose-tipped
globes rose and fell with the breathing of their owner.

The black African pushed himself up on one elbow. The salon of the sailboat seemed to be a waver-
ing sea of flesh. From his position, all he could see
were buttocks and breasts in a kaleidoscope of white,
black and tan.

Memory seeped back slowly as he felt himself
growing hard. He and Beck had decided to stay with
the boat when Alex and Billy Two took off to Alaska.

They thought they'd cruise the coast from Lauderdale to the Keys.

What they hadn't counted on was the boat's reputation. The female beach bums knew the boat was always good for food and drink and a satisfying roll in the hay. They hadn't made it to Miami before the steady stream of females began. They tried to keep it down to two or three, but soon they were overwhelmed by almost a dozen.

It was more than the two mercs could handle, although God knew they tried.

Hayes started to crawl carefully across the sea of brown and white in search of Beck. Hayes was a heavy, tall, well-muscled man who had been with the Navy SEALs and fought as an African freedom fighter. Beck was a little guy, a computer genius, but one hell of a fighter when the battle chips were down.

Right now, he was nowhere to be seen. Hayes bellowed cautiously, "Nate! Where the hell are you?"

Beck's face appeared next to a pair of white thighs, eyes bleary, hair tousled, the chin quivering with a happy look of indecision above a delicious pair of buttocks. He had a grin on his face. A grin that had grown somewhat weary since they left Key West.

They had to get out of there, put a stop to the cruise—and soon, Hayes thought. It had become a matter of survival.

As he stared at Beck, he heard their call sign come over the ship-to-shore radio. With difficulty Hayes pulled himself free from the undulating pile and, picking his feet carefully between the sated bodies, made his way to the map table.

He turned up the volume and pushed the Talk button. "Virtuous calling. Virtuous. Come in."

"That you, Claude?"

"Colonel? Thank God! Tell me you need us for a job. Please."

"Don't tell me you can't handle Nanos's overflow."

"Something like that."

"Get your ass out of there and wait for me at the Alaska Inn in Fairbanks. Nate with you?"

"Yeah. I just hope we've got the energy to pull our weight."

"You can ask Alex how he does it when you see him. See you there."

"Thanks, Colonel. We owe you one."

ON PETIT ST. VINCENT, Barrabas put down the phone. He enjoyed a private laugh at the plight of Hayes and Beck, but wasn't surprised. After all, they weren't in the same class as Nanos and Billy Two when it came to women. He could understand the deep-seated need that fueled his men's hunger. After one of their most suicidal jobs, it was hard not to succumb to the demands of the flesh and the bottle, as if to partake from either would be the last time. When he'd had Erika Dykstra as a friend and lover, the need to seek solace elsewhere never entered his mind. There was nothing strange about the fact that his soldiers looked for someone to hold onto between battles. It wasn't a compulsion—there were other things in life. But when memories of grenades exploding too close woke them from restless sleep, a warm body was better comfort than a bottle of pills or booze. He understood only too well.

He turned his mind back to the next job. Whatever the final plan for Alaska turned out to be, six of his people were already there or underway. O'Toole, the redheaded Irish-American, his right hand man, was in San Diego. After his meeting with Jessup, searching the bars for the former army captain wouldn't be a problem for Barrabas.

The Alaska setup carried strange vibrations all the way to his marrow. He had led the SOBs against tyrants of one kind or another in Iran, Africa, Russia, Cambodia and a dozen other places, but the struggle had now been taken to American soil. He'd gone with his crew to Florida to stop a group of terrorists from creating a bloody massacre. That had been on home soil. But there was something different about the new mission. An all-out battle against the Big Bear. No matter how well disguised, it was Ivan up to his old tricks. And this time it was against America.

That gave him more incentive. The last man out of Vietnam, Barrabas had fought and given his all for America, then vowed he'd only fight if he was paid for it. Yes, something was different. When he talked to Jessup, he'd have to be careful not to be undermined by his feelings. He couldn't sell his men's services cheaply

He's have to play it by ear.

He got up from his chair near the bar. He'd been alone while he made his phone calls, except for a beautiful island woman tidying up. She had looked him over shyly, seductively, while he'd talked. He was six-foot-four, broad shouldered. His short, prematurely white hair was an interesting contrast to the deep bronze of his tan. He looked rested and healthy. With only his trunks as covering, his well-muscled body was attractively displayed to any woman with a healthy appetite for life.

He was accustomed to women giving him a certain kind of look. But now was not the time or place. He was sated with the fulfilling companion he'd brought with him, physically and mentally. But more than that, he had a job to do.

He felt good. Not only was he getting back into action, but he would also be standing up for his country. He grinned at his own thoughts, his white teeth a sudden show of white at the woman clearing off the tables.

She swallowed and smiled, her eyes glazed with passion.

Barrabas flashed her an understanding look as he padded by on bare feet.

"Next time, baby. Maybe next time."

**6**

Billy Two sat cross-legged in front of the fire. Nanos sprawled on a bearskin rug with a full glass of Johnny Walker in one hand. Charlie sat between them in an old rocker, keeping it going, pushing off with one foot every few seconds.

"How much did Chank tell you about what he did with us, Charlie?" Nanos asked.

"Just about everything. He came back from Siberia, sat right there on that old bear rug and told me the whole gulag story... about the scientist, Billy getting left behind. He thought a lot about you, Billy."

Billy Two didn't respond. He didn't like to think back to the Russian Balandin and the drugs. He wasn't the man he'd been before the gulag job and his capture. Every day was an effort, and it worked best if he didn't dwell on that experience. He snapped out of his mood and looked at Charlie and Nanos. They seemed to be waiting for him to say something.

"Chank ever have any weapons here, Charlie?" he asked.

"Left everything he had to his girlfriends, except an old army barracks box." Charlie grinned mischievously. "Maybe you'd like to see it."

"The sneaky guy," Nanos chuckled. "Where is it?"

"Hang on a minute. I'll show you."

Charlie Dayo went to a sideboard and took an oil lamp from a shelf. He struck a kitchen match, pulled up the glass and lit the wick. It smoked at first, surrounding them with the smell of kerosene.

"Get off that bearskin, Alex. Pull on the ring in the floor, there."

Billy Two moved to where Nanos was looking and found a small ring recessed into the plank floor. The carpentry had been so good that the outline of the trapdoor was almost invisible. He reached for the ring and pulled. A door slid up easily. Stairs led below into a well of darkness.

Charlie led the way with the lamp. When he reached the bottom, he hung the lamp on a hook in the low ceiling and turned to a box in one corner. He took a key from his shirt, and after a moment of fumbling, opened the dusty box.

"Holy shit! Look at that, Billy!" Nanos exclaimed, reaching for a well-used M-16. He took it out, slid back the breech, and looked down the barrel. It was in perfect condition.

Billy ignored a second M-16 and picked up an Uzi automatic. Like the American-made guns, the small Israeli weapon was in perfect condition.

"Two M-16s, two Uzis," Billy said. "Extra clips, magazines and boxes of ammunition, some walkie-talkies. What the hell was he saving this for, Charlie?"

"Chank had a dark side, Billy," Charlie said, heading for the stairs. "Come on. Bring the stuff upstairs, and we can talk."

The hulking Indian picked up the heavily loaded box as though it was a case of beer and carried it up the narrow stairs.

"What do you mean, dark side?" Nanos asked when they were seated around a table, the guns in front of them.

"He brooded a lot. He told me he was going to die on the Majorca job with you guys, and he did." Charlie Dayo reached for his glass and drained it. "When you were taken, Billy, he thought you were dead and his luck had run out with you."

"Why the weapons?"

Charlie looked at them both. He wasn't smiling. "Maybe two reasons," he said. "This is a lonely outpost. Even with the oil people here, he wanted protection after he came back from the Marines. Chank was never the same after the war. Some kind of personal devil was after him, never gave him peace."

"That's one reason. What was the other?" Nanos asked.

"I'm not sure he'd want me to tell you," Charlie said.

"He wanted you to bury them with him. But we didn't bring his body home," Billy Two said, knowing Chank too well and guessing. They'd been somewhat kindred spirits.

"Is that right, Charlie?" Nanos asked. "You can tell us."

"Yeah. That's what he wanted."

Billy Two thought about the friend who had been ripped in two under the rubble of Lee Hatton's casa on the island of Majorca. When the body had been recovered, Barrabas had arranged for Chank's burial on the island.

"Chank will have friends to take care of him, wherever he went," he said, his eyes moist. The talk about Chank was making him maudlin.

"Were you in Vietnam, Charlie?" Nanos asked.

"Army. One hitch and out. No place for a man who likes to sleep under the stars with no sergeant's voice in a hundred miles."

"We could have more trouble here, Charlie. You with us in this?"

"You mean as an SOB?"

"No. That's up to the colonel. Just this place. Your place. The SOBs might be coming to Alaska, but the Soviets, or whoever the hell they are, might attack again."

"Here? Again! Shit! This is my home. If they come here, they'll have to get past me this time."

"Okay, Charlie. We'll set up watches. Get some new batteries for the walkie-talkies, and one of us sleeps on the point every night—or we all do."

"You really think they'll come back?" Charlie asked.

"The pipeline terminal is still intact. Our colonel thinks they'll be back to destroy it."

"Man. If they come, I'll be waiting, and I'll have the right weapon in my hand. Let the bastards come."

LE GOURMET WAS CROWDED when Barrabas stepped in from the street. The room was dim, lit by some spotlights recessed into the ceiling. Waiters in formal dress hovered over tables covered with the finest linen. A string quartet played softly on a podium in the corner farthest from the door.

The maître d' approached, eyeing Barrabas's blue shirt and jeans doubtfully. "Something I can do for you, sir?"

"Mr. Jessup's table."

"This way, sir," the head waiter said, an indifferent smile creasing his face as he led the tall man to a secluded booth.

The wide expanse of Jessup's backside took up half of the padded semicircular booth. The table was almost covered with dishes. A bottle of wine was chilling in an ice bucket at the fat man's side. The expression on his face was close to ecstasy. He raised a loaded fork to his cavernous mouth.

Looking up, he smiled with his mouth full. He nodded for Barrabas to sit.

The headwaiter returned with a menu and Barrabas waved him away.

"You're later than I thought," Jessup said, wiping his mouth with a linen napkin.

"Held up in St. Vincent. How far have we progressed?"

"To the main course. I'm having Arctic char. Appropriate, no?"

"How far have you progressed with the senator?"

"I've got a story to tell you, Nile," Jessup said, a smile stretching his wide face. He put down his fork and leaned on his elbows. "His secretary, Miss Roseline, has proved a valuable ally. I happened to meet her at a coffee shop. She told me a story she just couldn't keep to herself."

Jessup told Barrabas about the senator's run-in with the DCI. Another visit from the Secretary of Defense had gone much the same way. The senator wanted civilian use of military hardware, and the defense chief wanted no part of it. The senator had won his point.

"What did he ask for?" Barrabas asked.

"He got a blank check, for chrissakes." Jessup raised another forkful of fish to his mouth.

"He told the defense secretary we'd need the latest class of Coast Guard cutter. Several ships are already berthed at the Coast Guard station at Kodiak, waiting for you to make a choice."

"What about aircraft?"

"The base commander at Eielson Air Force Base has orders to provide a helicopter gunboat and anything else you need. He's already set up refueling stations along the coast." Jessup paused, raised a glass of white wine in a toast and drained it. "Eielson is a few miles southeast of Fairbanks," he went on. "Bishop can fly you to pick out the ship at Kodiak."

"A few things bother me about this job, Walker. We're coming out in the open. We need a lot of intelligence we can't gather ourselves. And we can't leave enemy bodies scattered over the landscape in our own backyard."

"The CIA is going to track enemy movements by spy satellite and report to the senator. They're going to send cleanup squads in your wake with an ample supply of body bags."

Jessup reached into a vest pocket and handed over a slip of paper. "Call that number day or night after a firefight, and the ghouls come out of the woodwork," he said.

"If the DCI can track the enemy, he can track us," Barrabas said, a frown creasing his handsome face.

"Like one big chess game," Jessup said, grinning.

"I don't like it. On a clear day, those satellite cameras can pick out facial features."

"So wear masks or something."

"I thought you and the senator wanted to keep us in the cold. I sure as hell like it better that way. The Florida job proved we'd be better off going in anonymously."

"Look," Jessup said, pushing his plate away. He waited while a waiter collected empty plates. "Try to keep your distance, okay? The DCI has been told the score. He's not going to be chafing at our heels."

"If it's the Russians, do we hit them as hard as last time?"

"This is our country and our people, Nile. You hit whoever is doing this as hard as necessary."

"Into their backyard, if necessary?"

"We'll have to get a better reading on that. In the meantime, the markings are being painted off military equipment. If you are caught, we don't know you. Nothing is changed."

"Nothing is changed, but everything is changed, goddammit. This is *our* country," Barrabas said.

"I couldn't agree more. But we're still not doing it for free, are we?"

"How much?" Barrabas asked.

"Considering the circumstances, five hundred thou a man. Okay?"

"Okay. That's it, then. I'll take a flight out of here tonight for San Diego."

"O'Toole?"

"The same."

"Give the big boozer my regards. He saved my ass once," Jessup said.

"And one hell of a big job that was, friend." Barrabas stood and walked away without looking back, glad to get away. He would have preferred another place for a meeting. Not that he disliked fancy restaurants when in the proper mood and with Erika or some other lovely on his arm. But with a fat man filling his face like a stoker, and with the business at hand, a beer in a tavern where men couldn't care less what was discussed at the other table would have suited Barrabas better.

Jessup sat back, satisfied in many ways. A man slipped quietly into the seat just vacated by Barrabas. Jessup recognized the type immediately. CIA.

"Remember Don Fairchild?" the man asked.

"Sure I remember him. How's the old bastard?"

Jessup was amused to see the young man cringe. He was tall, his features sharp, his hair worn short, almost in a brush cut. He looked like the early version of the men Hoover used to be surrounded with.

"He wants to see you. I have a car."

Alone in the back seat, Jessup watched familiar landmarks of Washington flash by, and eventually lost interest. Finally the car stopped alongside another under a bridge in total darkness.

The young man left. Someone opened the back door and slipped into the seat.

"It's been a long time, Walker," Don said, his voice holding a hint of amusement.

"A long time. I see you're still playing games."

"We're both in the business," Don said, the amused inflection still in his voice. "The pay's a little better the way you handle your end."

"So what's with the cloak and dagger tonight?" Jessup asked.

"The DCI would have my ass if he knew. I decided we were into something you had to know."

"Oh? Why isn't the DCI passing it along?"

"Don't be naive, Walker. My boss takes a lot of shit from people in power and then tells them what he wants them to know."

"So what is it he doesn't want us to know?"

"It's very important to you, isn't it?"

"How much?"

"Don't sound so sanctimonious," the CIA man said. "We all need money, right? Ten thousand."

"You don't know anything worth ten thousand. I'll give you one, just for old times' sake."

"Five. That's it," the CIA man said, looking around furtively as if expecting to see someone.

"Okay. So what's worth that much?"

"We picked up another former Greenpeace member. This one was given the full treatment. We learned a lot."

Jessup knew what the "full treatment" was. He also knew it wasn't any more humane than what the Russians employed when they had to. The intelligence would be reliable. "So tell me. What's so earth-shattering?"

"The French have paid a man named Beaudreau half a million dollars to discredit Greenpeace. Beaudreau's not been seen since."

"Is he working alone, or has he a sponsor?" Jessup asked.

"The man we had didn't know," Fairchild said. "Beaudreau was always a militant—always at odds with his Greenpeace bosses. The man who was killed in the Auckland bombing was a close friend of his. Beaudreau didn't blame the French. Figured it was Greenpeace stubbornness that cost him his friend's life."

Jessup's eyes became accustomed to the dark, and he could see his old friend quite well now. They were both a lot older. Fairchild's white hair curled around his soft felt hat. Lines streaked his face around his eyes and mouth. He looked used up, tired and at the end of the road. Espionage was a hard life.

"You were there, Don. What do you think?" Jessup asked.

"I don't think the man knew. He told us Beaudreau was greedy and shrewd. I think Beaudreau wouldn't want to spend any part of the half million to carry out a terrorist act if he could get someone else to finance it."

"I agree. So the Russians have a genuine front. The French have paid out hard cash."

"A perfect setup for the KGB if they get their hands on Beaudreau," Fairchild speculated.

"My guess is he went to them," Jessup said. "It was worth the five thousand. If you get more, we can do business."

"Could be," Fairchild chuckled as he slid from the seat, leaving as silently as he had come.

The young driver returned to his place behind the wheel and drove Jessup to the front of his residence as if he'd done it every night.

In the quiet of his apartment, Jessup didn't turn on the lights as he reached for the phone. He keyed in a number from memory and waited.

"Who is calling?" an indifferent voice asked.

"Walker Jessup. It's urgent."

A long silence followed before the familiar voice came on the line. "What is it?" the senator asked.

"Two things. The DCI is keeping you in the dark. They've interrogated another former Greenpeace member." He went on to tell the senator all he knew. "Second, I just had dinner with Barrabas. He's on his way. He asked a question, and I gave him a negative answer for now."

"I presume you're going to tell me," the senator said in his usual impatient manner.

"If the enemy is obviously Russian, does he follow them to their base?"

"You gave him the right answer. Let me know every step of the confrontation. We may change the order. Or we may back him up officially."

"I don't like having to deal with the military or the CIA. Too damned much jealousy between them all. Your DCI friend has proved that already."

"Leave him to me."

They rang off without further exchange, both men disturbed by the need for official liaison. Jessup recalled an old principle in dealing with officialdom: if anything could go wrong, it would.

## 7

General Boris Mesmerof sat in the back of the shiny black ZIL as it cruised almost silently through the Kremlin gate and into the inner courtyard. His driver had been to the old palace before. The man shared none of his inner anxiety about the visit, Mesmerof thought, stirring uneasily. The reasons for his fears were more imagined than real. He was the director of the First Chief Directorate of the KGB. A man of power, he was someone whom the irst Secretary would treat with respect. There was no need for fear.

As the ZIL approached the darkened portico, the general slipped to the side he would exit. A guard opened the door, stood back and saluted.

Like his right hand man, Petrov, Mesmerof preferred tailored suits with a military cut instead of the cardboard stiffness of the uniforms favored by his colleagues. His suit couldn't hide the excesses of his lifestyle, but it was an improvement over the attire of the old guard.

The walk to the first secretary's apartment was painful for Mesmerof. Angina grabbed his heart and hung on while he strove for normalcy before the guards who were posted at intervals and watched his progress. He wished he could stop for a nitro pill, but he couldn't.

After what seemed like miles, the huge carved doors of the first secretary's apartment loomed out of the gloom of the wide corridors. Two guards, seemingly alerted by his approach, demanded his identification.

The grossly overweight general was permitted into an inner sanctum where a secretary examined his party identification carefully. While that ceremony went on in the dim anteroom, Mesmerof pulled out a large white handkerchief and wiped his perspiring dome.

"You may go in those doors," the secretary finally said. "The first secretary is expecting you."

Mesmerof had known the first secretary for many years. They had never been close. The supreme Soviet leader was much younger, from the new breed, and not a man to dwell on acquaintances. He had always seemed cold, unbending and relentless. A stubborn man, he was used to getting his own way.

Mesmerof approached the far end of the room where the man sat in a deep wing chair before a roaring, open fire. The place where the Soviet leader spent most of his time was the most luxuriously decorated room in the Kremlin. He was in his early fifties, of middle height and weight. His face was round, the body doughy, though not fat. Sparse hair was combed across his bald pate, partly hiding a birthmark that was a brown streak across the side of his skull. The man, who seldom smiled, got to the point disturbingly fast.

"General, sit and pour yourself some coffee." There had been no warmth in the invitation.

Mesmerof would have liked a Scotch or two, but knew how the first secretary felt about drinking. Since his campaign to reduce alcoholism started, the man hadn't taken a drink.

"Tell me about the Greenpeace affair. Was the first strike effective?" he asked.

Mesmerof had discussed the plan with the first secretary before going ahead with it. After Petrov had displayed such a negative attitude, he had begun to have doubts and had approached the country's top man with trepidation. But the supreme leader of the Soviets had been more enthusiastic than Mesmerof or his boss, the head of the KGB. Mesmerof had explained that certain KGB and Politburo members felt the plan was dangerous, but the first secretary thought a lot of progress would be made, without anybody tracing the attacks to the USSR.

"There are still rumbles of fear about striking on American soil, despite the use of foreign mercenaries," Mesmerof warned, covering himself.

"We've already gone over that ground. Tell me about the first strike."

"Good and bad, First Secretary. The Yupiks planted the charges, but the foreign material exploded prematurely, and the Americans were roused before our men were clear."

"Any of our people captured?"

"No. We recovered every one."

"So the pipeline is destroyed."

"Not exactly. Most of the derricks are down and the majority of the pumps are out of commission. But the pipeline terminal is still intact."

The reaction was swift and violent. The first secretary threw his coffee cup at the fireplace, smashing it against the stone. A stain crept slowly from one piece of rock to the next.

"You will stick to the plan, General. The pipeline terminal, then the rigs offshore in the Beaufort Sea, then the experimental station."

He slammed his fist on the table beside his chair. "It should have been so easy. We could have dealt them a blow three times before they knew what had hit them."

"With all respect, First Secretary," General Mesmerof said as calmly as he could. He was sweating profusely, and the fire wasn't helping. "The ships are slow and old. The men are not of our military. All the weapons are of foreign manufacture. Should we plan on more attacks? No one will blame the French or Greenpeace."

"Those are but weak excuses, and you know it!" the most powerful man of the USSR shouted. "Get the job done, General. Get it done without it pointing to us. Discredit the French—just do it—whatever it takes."

"Yes, First Secretary," Mesmerof blubbered as he prepared to leave, knowing the interview was over.

"And Mesmerof," the man in the high-back chair said coldly. "Make it work, or you won't have to worry about a bypass. You won't have time."

As he left, Mesmerof's perspiration turned into cold sweat. That devil knew everything. How the hell—the doctor? It didn't matter. It was a lever he'd have to live with.

**8**

A cold wind whistled in from the Beaufort Sea. The sun had gone down, but a full moon bathed the stark landscape with a mellow light. Alex Nanos pulled the loose sealskins around him as he sat at the end of the easterly point of Prudhoe Bay. The smell of gutted fish was strong, mixed with the constant smell of oil from the pumps inland.

He didn't much care for times like these when a man had nothing to do but think. He'd rather have his hands on a soft round body than the stalk of an M-16. Kaweetha. Now there was a body. The only woman he'd ever had whom he couldn't best in bed. Each night when he'd been with her, he'd felt as though she'd had him instead of the other way around.

From where he lay, he'd watched the Inupik men push off in their boats in the morning and return at night, and they reminded him of his father. When he was a kid in Florida, he'd watched his father go out for fish and had wanted to go with him. When he'd grown and his father wanted him to work the boats, he'd been too wrapped up in his own life. When he should have joined the old man, it was time to join the military.

He remembered meeting Billy Two on the day of their discharge, on the Oakland Ferry. They'd been close ever since, sharing good and bad. In some ways, he wished he was more like Billy. The big Osage wanted nothing more than to be an Indian of the plains, but he'd been born too late for that.

A dark blob materialized on the horizon. It came closer and took on shape.

Nanos didn't overreact. He had plenty of time. If it was the phony *Rainbow Warrior*, it had to come toward shore a long way before its boats would be lowered.

He picked up the Bell & Howell glasses Charlie had lent him. The hull almost jumped out at him as he focused. He could see one thing clearly on the hull—the large white dove near the bow.

She drifted closer, her screws turning slowly. Nanos estimated she would let her raiding party off in about an hour. He reached for his walkie-talkie, thumbed the Talk pad and whispered into the mike.

"Billy. Do you read?"

No answer. The big Indian was not only as big as a bear, he slept like one.

"Charlie. Do you read?"

"Alex? What's going down?"

"The big ship is coming in slowly," he whispered. "We use plan one, okay?"

"I'll wake the big guy, and we'll get in position. And Alex, give the bastards hell."

"You got it."

Alex the Greek left his radio on Receive and settled down to watch. When the boats were lowered, he'd signal, then move around the point to the beach and wait in position. Billy was to take up his post at the other end of the beach, with Charlie in the middle.

Nanos had set the strategy. He wanted a field of fire that would have the two SOBs bracketing the target at about a ninety-degree angle with their 5.56 NATO rounds. Charlie's job was to spray 9 mm slugs with the Uzis at the incoming boats. Unfamiliar with Charlie's skill, Nanos wanted the Eskimo to have both Uzis ready for firing without the need to reload right away. Having Charlie in the enemy's direct line of fire wasn't a problem. Nanos and Billy Two would keep the bastards so busy they wouldn't have time to worry about Charlie.

As he pondered his moves, the big ship began to steer to starboard, heading farther up the coast toward Simpson Lagoon.

He thumbed the Talk pad of the radio. "Charlie. You see them heading to your left?"

"Yeah."

"Okay. We drift with them. You with us, Billy?"

"I can see the action. I'm maintaining position. You'd better move your ass, Greek boy."

Nanos pulled the radio's sling over his shoulder, pushed the fur robes aside and started out at a crouch down the point and around the beach. He stopped and raised his glasses. He could see Billy Two in position and Charlie between them.

He swung the glasses toward the boat. She was a mile out, and her rainbow marking was easy to see. The inflatables had been lowered. He counted four boats, three or four men to a boat.

He thumbed the Talk pad again. "Last transmission. They are in the water. Four boats, about a dozen men. Keep low and open fire on my signal. Out."

The Russians came on, their outboards muffled. He could see the outline of the men: one at the tiller, two in front, a dozen in all. Billy Two would take out the boat closest to him. Alex would do the same. Charlie would spray the other two, and then they'd assess the damage—plan one.

Nanos didn't like the waiting game in battle. He never had. He preferred a quick and hot firefight with little time to think.

They were almost within range. He waited.... Soon they would be close enough.

When the portside boat was less than one hundred yards away, he opened up with a short burst. He heard the spitting of Uzi, as if it were answering the chatter of his weapon, but was unaware of the enemy returning fire.

His target boat was hit. He could hear the solid chunk as his slugs hit human flesh. Men thrashed about in the frigid water. Nanos had taped two cartridge cases together like a Mag-Pac. Now he flipped

# Terrorists, anarchists, hijackers and drug dealers—BEWARE!

In a world shock-tilted by terror, Mack Bolan and his courageous combat teams, *SOBs* and our new high-powered entry, *Vietnam: Ground Zero* provide America's best hope for salvation.

Fueled by white-hot rage and sheer brute force, they blaze a war of vengeance against a tangled international network of trafficking and treachery. Join them as they battle the enemies of democracy in timely, hard-hitting stories ripped from today's headlines.

## Get 4 explosive novels delivered right to your home—FREE

Return the attached Card, and we'll send you 4 gut-chilling, high-voltage Gold Eagle novels—FREE!

If you like them, we'll send you 6 brand-new books every other month to preview. Always before they're available in stores. Always at a hefty saving off the retail price. Always with the right to cancel and owe nothing.

As a subscriber, you'll also get…
- our free newsletter *AUTOMAG* with each shipment
- special books to preview and buy at a deep discount

## Get a digital quartz calendar watch—FREE

As soon as we receive your Card, we'll send you a digital quartz calendar watch as an outright gift. It comes complete with long-life battery and one-year warranty (excluding battery). *And like the 4 free books, it's yours to keep even if you never buy another Gold Eagle book.*

## RUSH YOUR ORDER TO US TODAY.

PRINTED IN U.S.A.

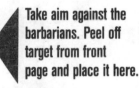

## Meet America's most potent human weapons

*Mack Bolan* and his courageous combat squads—
*Able Team & Phoenix Force*— along with *SOBs*
and *Vietnam: Ground Zero* unleash the best
sharpshooting firepower ever published.
Join them as they blast their way through page
after page of raw action toward a fiery climax
of rage and retribution.

out the empty side and reversed it in a hurry, shooting at the heads bobbing in the water.

The two boats in the middle had reversed and were starting to head back. One man jumped up, then fell backward into the water.

Suddenly a steel-hulled inboard raced from the ship and began to pick up enemy troops floundering in the Arctic water. Nanos had expected some heavy firepower from the mother ship, but not this. He thumbed the radio Talk pad.

"Billy. Use the FN SS109 rounds we found. Let's see if they'll penetrate the speedboat hull."

"Gotcha."

Nanos threw down the Mag-Pac and slammed in the new ammo. The sailors were having a hell of a time hauling bodies out of the drink. He concentrated his fire in 3-round bursts at the thwarts, scything down the rescue crew. They flew from the boat or lay dead across the thwarts.

When he changed magazines again, he heard the 9 mm off to his left. Charlie was busy with the Uzis.

Now the action had changed. One of the inflatables was out of range. Three had been hit and sunk as the outboards pulled the deflated dinghies to the bottom.

Nanos kept up a steady hail of steel at the rescue boat. The SOB fire had been devastating, but somehow the survivors were underway. Soon they would be out of range.

Nanos ran toward Charlie Dayo. The Eskimo had stopped firing and watched the rescue boat, which was now out of range. Billy jogged back along the beach.

Lights had gone on in the houses at Deadhorse. The chatter of anxious voices carried on the offshore breeze.

The sea told them nothing. The smell of fish and oil had been replaced by cordite and blood. And that would dissipate, too, with the steady lapping of the waves and the unceasing stirring of air over the waters.

As the three warriors converged, a man struggled through the waves, holding his shoulder. He was short and stocky.

They raced toward him, guns leveled. He collapsed facedown in the water.

AT CHARLIE'S CABIN, Alex Nanos left the Inuit to render first aid and interrogate their prisoner. He was worried about the bodies washing ashore down the beach. The colonel had given him a number to call. He walked to the hotel, away from everyone, to make his call on a phone in the small lobby.

"Yeah" was all the person at the other end said.

"Town of Deadwood. Up the beach toward the west."

"How many?" The question was terse and without emotion.

"Not sure. It was dark. Invaders in rubber dinghies. Between six and nine should wash ashore."

"What about the locals?"

"They've been kept clear."

"We come in quietly and we leave quietly. No witnesses. That includes you."

Nanos hung up without comment. Cold bastards, he thought. Well, they had a job to do. And who the hell was he to think of them as ghouls?

## 9

Liam O'Toole was under assault, and he wasn't doing anything to prevent it. He'd been shacked up with the muscular blonde for a week at a tavern and motel called The Mercenary, and she'd about worn him out. She was a dancer, a mud wrestler, a woman with almost limitless endurance and a groupie. Right now, with Rambo, Chuck Norris and *The Terminator* showing on the big screen everywhere, she was a camp follower, a lover of mercs.

She had raved over the big redhead's six-foot-two frame. It was not the hard slabs of muscle that had turned her on, but the scars she found in abundance. Every time they got into bed, she traced her fingers over the scars and then, driven by a lust she couldn't control, worked her hands over his body.

O'Toole wasn't with it this time. While she sought her own pleasure, he thought about the wars he'd been in, the jobs with Barrabas and the others. He tried to shut out all thoughts about the treachery of his bride and the drama of their parting, but they crept in, even at times like this. Whenever he looked in the mirror and saw the puckered flesh from the wound in his shoulder, he could see her holding the gun.

Right now he was bored. A strong young woman was straining herself to arouse him, and he was bored. He was physically excited—she'd made sure of that. But he couldn't get his mind in tune with the rod of flesh she was using for her own pleasure. It seemed as though his mixed-up head was detached from his body.

Finally he started to bring his mind in line. The random thoughts disappeared, and he felt a rush of passion spread through his loins. From there, as with any man, nature took over.

As he moved, he could feel the woman increase her efforts, match his pace and pick up the tempo, straining for yet another wave of delight to consume her.

It was getting closer. The smell of her attacked him, the female sweat, wafting her damp warmth. Sensation rushed at him. He raced with it, his heart pumping wildly in a final burst of ecstasy.

He needed release between firefights. It was booze, women or poetry. He spent little time putting pen to paper. He had almost ruined his life with booze. So it had to be women, or else a kind of inner madness brought back the nightmares of battle. He often wondered whether other mercs were the same. He never talked about it.

He felt the full-length softness of her, her warmth as she collapsed on him. She wanted to cling, to make it last, but it was over. He slipped from her and headed for the shower, realizing the whole shackup was finished. He poured three fingers of Bushmills in a plastic cup and took it with him.

When he had dressed, he downed another shot of the Irish firewater and called to her.

"I'm going to the bar. Come on over when you're ready."

He closed the door of the motel room behind him and headed across a square of cracked asphalt to the darkened bar.

The motel and bar was off Highway 8, close to Allied Gardens, maybe thirty miles northeast of San Diego. It had been opened by an old-time merc who had been shot up one time too many. Most vehicles in the parking area were pickups belonging to the local boys, each sporting a rifle and a shotgun on a rack behind the driver.

O'Toole pushed open the swinging doors and entered the bar. The walls were covered with guns, old and new. All had been rendered harmless, but as decoration they were effective. Battered helmets and armor hung from the ceiling, accented by psychedelic lights. Pictures of famous mercs adorned the area around the bar. The place smelled of beer and unwashed bodies. The locals were vocal. They had an undying thirst. But they seemed to have an aversion to soap and water.

Wild Bill, the owner, was polishing glasses behind the counter. He waved at O'Toole, poured a Bushmills and put it in front of him. He knew who O'Toole was, and it amused him to see the way the big Irish-American took the snide remarks of the phonie. Bill knew who the real men were—the fighting men who came to him from around the world.

"How you been, Liam? That woman bothering you? Want me to chase her?"

"She's all right. Too acrobatic for this old man, but she's okay."

"Good crowd tonight."

"Where the hell do they all come from, Bill?" O'Toole waved an arm.

"Hey, don't knock it. These crazies used to go up the road to the Rodeo Club. They got bucking-horse machines to ride up there and cowboy women. *Rambo* changed all that, thank God. This place used to be a morgue at night."

"Hey, Red! How about a poem?" one of the locals called out. He was a skinny blond kid with acne, dressed in fatigues, paratrooper boots and a jungle hat, all fresh from the war surplus store.

"Yeah. Come on, Red," some of the others chorused.

"Don't let those pricks get to you, Liam. If I fired off a few rounds, they'd shit their pants."

O'Toole smiled down at the old warrior. "A poet never passes up an audience, Bill. Got to let your talent show, right?"

O'Toole stepped to a podium in the center of the room and flicked on the small spot. He sat on a high bar stool and looked down at the grinning young faces. Before he started, he pondered a truth that had been sneaking up on him lately: the faces in bars were looking younger to him—always younger.

The woman who had been living with him for a week stepped through the swinging doors into the room and stood silently waiting for the action, hands on her hips. She was a good-looking woman, he thought as he began.

A body crisscrossed with scars
Tells its own story.

The woman, as if anticipating, moved to the podium and sat at his feet.

A knife slash here,
A puncture there.

The woman slid her hands up his body as he spoke, pulling his shirt from his pants and over his head. The scores of white shiny slashes and zippers of flesh, unevenly stitched, stood out against his tanned hide. The puckered bullet wound he'd taken in Northern Ireland caught the light like a cut-glass stone in a stripper's navel.

Knives unsheathed,
Guns used in war,
Rip at soft flesh.

The woman slid off his shoes, unbuckled his belt, pulled down his zipper and eased his pants down. Ugly ridges of scar tissue stood out against brown skin.

Wars since time began,
Wars that have been
And will be again.
They kill and maim.

The woman slid his pants from under his feet. Wild Bill tore an M-10 from the wall and a bullet-riddled helmet from the ceiling. He handed them to her. She put the gun in O'Toole's hands and the metal hat on his head.

The podium rotated.

No one spoke.

The silence was absolute.

Wear the clothes of war.
Shout the slogans.
Then, you mothers of sin,
Go out and die.

The silence remained.

O'Toole stood, naked except for the thin scrap of bikini shorts, the story of battle etched on his skin, the gun held ready, his face a mask.

A tall white-haired man was standing just inside the door, a witness to O'Toole's story. Through the frozen silence, Barrabas called.

"Liam O'Toole! It's time!"

FOR A BIG MAN, Jessup had moved faster than any of them. He had reserved the largest suite the Alaska Inn had and was set up for the others when they arrived.

Early in the day after the second attack on Deadhorse, they sat around his suite, with coffee and doughnuts laid on. The room was huge, papered in gold flocking. Three crystal chandeliers hung from the ornately plastered ceiling. It contained four sofas and six easy chairs, but Jessup had ordered a conference table and ten leather swivel chairs set up. The smell of coffee filled the air around them.

"Colonel, did anyone tell you Alex finally met his match in Alaska?" Billy Two asked.

"You sic that bear on him, Billy?" Hayes asked, remembering his one other trip to the forty-ninth state.

"Hey. Kaweetha was a very nice lady," Nanos countered. "We shouldn't be talking about her, right?"

"Wrong," Beck said. "You been flaunting your women in front of us for years. Tell us about her, Billy."

"More than a hundred pounds of muscle and very talented," Billy said. "From what I hear. And I don't mean words."

"Look at those two." Nanos pointed at Hayes and Beck across the table from him. "Looks like they're about to come apart at the seams from trying to satisfy my friends in Florida."

Barrabas listened for a few minutes, looking around the table at the whole team. Hatton and Bishop had flown in yesterday. They both looked relaxed, ready for the job. Nanos was right about Hayes and Beck. They did look a little ragged around the edges. He and O'Toole had flown up from San Diego together, and the big redhead had slept all the way. Jessup was busy, as usual, consuming doughnuts—two bites for each.

"Tell us about your prisoner," he asked, turning to Alex Nanos.

"Interesting story, Colonel. An Eskimo with a Russian name. Josef Garin. His people are Yupik Eskimo, originally from our side, just north of the Aleutians. When we bought Alaska from the Russians, some of the Yupiks were trapped on the Chukchi Peninsula over there." He sipped his coffee.

"Where is he?" Barrabas asked.

"In my room, Colonel," Billy said. "Charlie Dayo's with him. We need Charlie as interpreter."

"Does the Russian know anything?"

"He's got to know where their base is, how many ships, personnel, things like that," Nanos said.

"Okay. We keep him close. Charlie will have to open him up," Barrabas said. "But, make one thing clear, Alex, and you too, Billy. Charlie may know a lot about us because of Chank, but he's not part of this operation. Just an interpreter. Got it?"

They both nodded.

"Okay," Barrabas continued. "We're here because the Russians are using the Greenpeace organization as a blind to damage our oil resources up here. They've attacked the north shore at Deadhorse twice. The first time, they did a lot of damage to the oil field. They killed about thirty Americans.

"The second time, Billy and Nanos fought them off and took one prisoner. That's about it up to now."

"What about Charlie spotting the French flag? Did you see it, Alex?"

"Too dark. But I believe Charlie," Nanos said. "That gives us several scenarios. First, it could be a totally French operation. Second, the French could have decided to discredit the Greenpeace people after the Auckland affair, and the Russians got into it somehow. And last, it could be a Russian plot, and they're using the French as a blind."

"Which do you think it is?" Barrabas asked.

"I'd bet my shirt the Russians are into it somehow," Jessup said. "It's not just prejudice, but can you see the French attacking our oil installations?"

"I agree with Jessup," Lee Hatton said. "But isn't there a chance they'll give it up now, Colonel? They've got to know their Greenpeace charade is over."

"The CIA believe the Russians will press this thing further," Jessup spoke up. "They only needed the veneer of Greenpeace to get it started. They'll play it as far as they can, believing we won't send in our military." He filled his mouth with a cream doughnut, downed it with coffee and went on, white powder surrounding his mouth. "They think the Russians are supporting a former Greenpeace member who's gone sour and is being paid by the French. I'll know tomorrow."

Bishop changed the subject. "A hell of a lot of territory to cover here, Colonel," he said.

"Our biggest problem, Geoff." He swung his head slowly around, looking each one in the eye. "This is a first for us. First time to defend American soil—except for the Florida job, but that was against terrorists and not the Soviets. First time we've been substituted for what should be a massive search and destroy force."

"The President just won't permit our military to officially engage the Russians," Jessup said. "We have the services of the CIA and the military, thanks to the senator."

"Yahoo!" Billy Two broke the mood. "We should order up a battleship. You handle a battleship or a carrier, Alex?" he asked.

"Anything that floats, Billy," the Greek answered, a grin splitting his handsome face.

"We can get down to that kind of detail," Jessup said. "I've been in touch with the Coast Guard station at Kodiak and the Eielson Air Force Base just south of us."

He drained his coffee and poured another cup. "We have to decide what we need."

"We've got to patrol the air- and sea-lanes," Barrabas said. "The CIA is supplying Walker with satellite photos of the region on a regular basis. He will stay here as our war room, study the photos and keep us posted. We will split into two groups and patrol until we have a target.''

"What do the Air Force have for me, Jessup?" Bishop asked.

"Quite an assortment. They're using this base to test some foreign equipment."

"Like what?" the Canadian pilot asked.

"Would you believe a British Ferranti attack helicopter, or an Italian Managusta? You also have a choice of the new Bell 222 that's been set up for long-range patrol, an experimental McDonnell Apache or a Huey," Jessup replied.

"What about a fighter if we need one?" Bishop asked.

"F-16s with long-range pods, data processing pods, AIM-9Js, radar-controlled missiles, whatever."

"I'll go over there when we're finished here. Probably use the new Bell 222. It's the fastest, can carry all of us, and it's long-range. We'll arm it ourselves," Bishop said.

"Better have an F-16 available, too, Geoff," Barrabas suggested.

"No way I'm going to pass that up, Colonel."

"All right. Let's complete the aircraft plans. You'd better have Nate with you as your computer man. Can you handle that, Nate?" Barrabas asked.

"Sounds good to me."

"The rest of us, Liam, Lee, Claude, Alex and Billy—we take to the sea. Alex will be captain with

Claude as first officer." He stopped again to let it sink in. "Any questions?"

"What's available for me, Colonel?" Nanos asked.

"Jessup?" Barrabas prompted.

"I talked to the Coast Guard, and we've got to remember that we aren't the Navy. Okay?" He put down the doughnut he was working on, wiped his hands and consulted his notes.

"Four choices. A 310-foot ship, one at 210 and one at about 80 feet," Jessup said.

"The biggest would be useless to us," Nanos said. "They take more than a hundred crew to operate, at least twenty for a skeleton crew. The eighty-footer would work, but it will have a couple of 50 mm at the most. It would be either twin diesel or twin gas turbine. Maybe twenty knots, tops."

He stopped and thought about it for a few seconds. "I'd like to cover a lot of water, and when we catch up to them, be able to sail circles around them," Nanos added, as if to himself. Then he looked up at Jessup. "You said four choices. What's the fourth?"

"An experimental one from the British. A Hovercraft. A big brute at about a hundred feet."

"Bingo! We can handle that," Nanos said. "Need to arm her. But we can pick up some rockets and cannon. Should be lots of places for mounts."

"Won't she be vulnerable, Nate?" Lee asked. "Big rubber pontoons vulnerable to firepower?"

"They're self-sealing," the Greek said, grinning in anticipation. "Look, this baby will go anywhere, through any seas, and at more than fifty knots. Just what we need.''

"Okay. It's settled. We can't spend any more time on this." Barrabas turned to Jessup. "Walker, call the two bases. Tell them to start their paint jobs, and Geoff will be over to the air base soon. He'll fly us down to Kodiak, so we have to wait for the helicopter."

"Do we really have carte blanche on this, Colonel?" Bishop asked.

"Right to the top. The commanding officers at the base know it."

"Then Nate and I should leave right now. Okay?" He looked at Lee as he spoke. It was a silent goodbye before battle. They would not be fighting side by side this time around.

As Bishop opened the door to leave, Charlie was about to knock. He came in, pulling the wounded Yupik after him. He motioned to Billy and whispered in his ear.

"The prisoner has been giving us some gems, Colonel," Billy said. "Maybe we'd better talk about it."

"Bring him in," Barrabas said and turned to help himself to a doughnut.

Charlie led the Russian prisoner in. "It's been a bitch communicating with him, Colonel," he said. "But I have some interesting answers!"

"Sit them down, Billy," Barrabas commanded. "Give them some coffee and doughnuts."

The Yupik had looked around the group with fear in his eyes. The wound in his shoulder had been dressed, and his arm was in a white sling that contrasted with his black fatigues. Salt from his dip in the cold Arctic sea had dried and crusted in white rings around his legs and arms. Looking very much like Charlie, he was stocky and well-muscled. He had long black hair and dark eyes. He kept his mouth clamped shut.

"What has he told you, Charlie?" Barrabas asked.

"A lot, Colonel. How long they trained. How many ships. That kind of thing."

"Ships? More than one? How many?"

"He says two. Both converted trawlers like the real Greenpeace."

"How are they armed?"

"Rocket launchers, 60 mm machine guns. All French-made and hidden under canvas."

"What is the ship's complement?"

"What's that, Colonel?" Charlie asked, taking a bite of chocolate doughnut that smeared his lips.

"How many men on the ships? How many trained as landing parties?"

Charlie exchanged words with the Russian Eskimo for a minute and turned back. "He says a skeleton crew of ten runs each ship. They were hired by a Frenchman, not by the Russians—mostly French and Algerians. Seagoing mercenaries. They have two assault forces to each ship, ten men to an assault force, all Yupiks."

"Where is their base?" Barrabas asked.

"Chukchi Peninsula. A fishing village named Inchoun."

Barrabas consulted one of his maps. Inchoun was only ten miles from the tip of the peninsula and Bering Strait. At that point, Bering Strait was only fifty miles across.

"Ask him where the military bases are."

"I did, Colonel. They have radar bases all along the coast to track incoming aircraft and missiles. But the air force and army bases are all inland."

"Last question. What in hell are these bastards up to?"

Charlie Dayo grimaced unpleasantly. "It's scary, Colonel Barrabas. Two ships, two more raids." He gestured toward the prisoner. "He says his boat's going to hit the research station on the National Petroleum Reserve east of Point Barrow six days from now. The other ship's heading south. Where to and what for—he doesn't know. And we don't have a hoot in hell of finding out. At least—before they hit us."

## 10

Colonel Alexi Petrov stood in front of Mesmerof's desk at rigid attention. It was late. Mesmerof was weary. He desperately didn't need to be between the wrath of the first secretary and the failure of his people. What he needed was rest and an end to it all.

"Sit down, Alexi," he said. "Take some Scotch."

He watched his tall and handsome deputy sit and pour with a steady hand. The old guard confronted by the new. This also wearied the old general.

"So we have failed once again," he said without anger. It was too late for him to play the old lion. He would do only what he had to.

"They were waiting for us, General."

"You get your information from Beaudreau," Mesmerof said calmly. "Mine tells me there were only three men on that shore."

"Three or a hundred. Without the element of surprise, it was an impossible task."

"We have two strikes left, and they must work. So this is what you are going to do."

He told Petrov it was his job to bird-dog the last two assaults from an observation helicopter and make sure both sorties were successful. Petrov had to ensure nothing fell into the hands of the Americans, even if it meant using his electronic detonators to blow their own people out of the water.

"I could be shot down by their aircraft if I fly into their airspace," Petrov protested.

"This has got to work, Alexi. You know I have loved you almost as a son."

"No helicopter has the range . . ."

"Refuel in the air. I don't want excuses. And one last thing," he said. "I suggest you carry no identification."

"What you're asking is suicide," Petrov complained.

The old general looked at him through eyes that were just slits. "We all had to earn our way. I've been in worse spots."

"This is a plan to get rid of me," the younger man shouted, losing control.

"Don't be a fool. Go and do your job like a man." He waved the younger man to the door in dismissal, knowing he probably wouldn't see him again.

The old man felt so tired. His chest was like a vise. For the first time in his career, Mesmerof questioned what it was all for. What had it given him but pain? He reached for the Scotch and the oblivion it offered.

BARRABAS STOOD IN THE WHEELHOUSE of the Hovercraft, next to Nanos. Bishop had flown them out of Fairbanks in the helicopter. They had arrived in Ko-

diak and taken a full day to mount four 50 mm machine guns and two Israeli manufactured Barak-1
antiaircraft missile systems, each with a magazine of
ten canisters. The Barak system was small and deadly,
effective against ships or aircraft.

Kodiak harbor was far behind them, and they were
cruising the light chop at more than fifty knots. The
huge propeller, mounted aft, was incredibly loud.
Fans beneath the floor provided the cushion of air the
Hovercraft rode on, adding to the noise and vibration.

Inside the wheelhouse Barrabas was able to talk to
Nanos without shouting, but the others, training with
Hayes on deck, had to huddle together to communi-
cate.

Alex Nanos kept one eye on his charts while watching the shoreline slipping by to starboard. They had
passed Koniuji Island south of Kodiak, heading for
the narrows in the Aleutian chain south of Unimak
Island about two hundred miles to the west. It was
cold, about thirty-five degrees Fahrenheit. The sea was
relatively calm, winds no more than ten knots.

"What's your ETA for the channel, Alex?" Barrabas asked.

"Four hours, Colonel. We'll be in the outer reaches
of Bristol Bay and free to head north. What's the latest from Bishop?"

"He's cruised the Beaufort Sea east and west of
Deadhorse. No sign of a Greenpeace ship or anything
suspicious."

"Maybe he'd better head south toward us."

"He's refueling at Point Barrow right now. He'll head south when he's airborne."

"Jesus, Colonel. We could be in this one over our heads. It's almost twelve hundred miles from the lower end of Bristol Bay to his position and a thousand miles from our position by sea." Nanos glanced at the chart again, checking for shoals, and went on. "We make a little better than fifty knots, and he covers about two hundred miles an hour. That's with the best equipment we can get."

"I know. The enemy could move in, strike a target and get out before we even get close."

"Any word from Jessup? The satellite pictures could be our ace in the hole."

"Nothing yet. He's got the first set of prints, and he's going over them now," Barrabas said.

Claude Hayes opened a hatch and stepped into the wheelhouse.

"How's the training?" Barrabas asked.

"We concentrated on ditching procedures."

"What's the drill?" Barrabas asked.

Nanos had them in open water. He took his eyes from the course to concentrate on his first officer.

"One lifeboat on the port side and one to starboard. Two-hundred-horse inboard motors with about eight hours of running time. Emergency rations and supplies."

"Easy to launch?" Barrabas asked.

"Best I've ever seen. One simple operation, takes a few seconds."

"Hydraulic?" Nanos asked.

"With manual backup. If the power's gone, you crank like hell."

As he spoke, the ship-to-shore radio squawked out their call signal.

Hayes grabbed for it. "Go ahead, Fairbanks."

"This is Jessup. Is Nile there?"

"Claude Hayes, Walker. I'm in the wheelhouse with Nanos and the colonel. I'm putting you on broadcast so we can all hear."

"Listen up," Jessup said. "I've spotted one of your phony ships just south of Nunivak Island."

"Where is that exactly?" Barrabas asked, spreading out a map.

"Bristol Bay is the whole body of water north of the Aleutian Islands and south of the Russian ship's position."

"Okay. I've got the island," Barrabas said. "It's about . . . four hundred miles north of the channel we plan to use to enter Bristol Bay, and we're more than three hours from the channel. That's a lot of time for them to roam. Are they heading south?"

"My photos show them heading south, but my photos are three hours old."

"Just a minute, Jessup," Barrabas said. He turned to Nanos. "Where would that put them?"

The Greek body builder, the best seaman and navigator on the team, looked at the map and put his finger on a spot in the middle of Bristol Bay. "Assuming they can't do better than twenty knots and the pictures are three hours old, they could be in the middle of Bristol Bay and only seven hours from us."

"Could the old ship be souped-up?" Barrabas asked.

"I doubt it," Nanos said. "They'd have to reinforce her hull. One hell of a lot of work."

"We'd better get Geoff and Nate down here fast. Walker, what do we have in Bristol Bay besides fish? My map shows no military targets."

"My pictures show five offshore oil derricks. I remember the controversy over them two years ago. A lot of environmental flak."

"Holy hell, Colonel," Nanos said. "That's it! The bastards can really give us some shit if they take out the offshore rigs."

"Jessup. You still with us?"

"I can hear it all. What do you want me to do?"

"Get another set of pictures immediately. I'm going to get on the horn with Geoff." Barrabas feared for the worst. "Get back to us as soon as you know anything else, Jessup. Claude. Get Geoff on the blower. We've got to get some firepower down here fast."

The big black man keyed in the frequency. "I've got Geoff for you, Colonel."

"Put him on the loudspeaker."

"Colonel." Bishop's voice came in loud and clear. "I'm just airborne from Point Barrow. What's the drill?"

"How fast can you get to the midpoint of Bristol Bay?"

A few seconds of silence followed then. "Nate's figuring it, Colonel. What's up?"

"The Russians have one of their Greenpeace boats in Bristol Bay right now. We have to intercept, but we're at at least six hours away. A lot of offshore oil stuff close to their position."

"Okay. Here it is. Six hours, plus a refueling at a place called St. Mary's. Call it six and a half if we're lucky."

"Shit!" Barrabas shouted in frustration. "The bastards can do a lot of damage in six hours."

"Time to call in the Air Force, Colonel?" Nanos asked.

"No can do, Alex. But you've given me an idea. You listening, Geoff?"

"Five by five, Colonel."

"Radio Eielson for your F-16. Have it on the tarmac at St. Mary's, fueled and ready when you get there."

"We won't lose her, Alex. We can't. Jessup can pick her up on satellite for us every few hours."

Walker wasn't the only one who recalled the environmental controversy over the offshore rigs. An oil spill or a blowout would kill off the salmon spawning throughout the bay and ruin fishing for the natives, perhaps permanently.

The chase was on, and with it the rising tension of approaching battle.

THE STOCKY FRENCHMAN STOOD at the helm of the old trawler as the others prepared to take off. He had ordered the old ship slowed to two knots. They coasted through the black water slowly as their rubber dinghies prepared to leave.

"I don't like this," he spoke to the first mate in French. "I haven't liked it from the start. Those damned oil rigs are American. All hell can break loose any minute."

"Remember the hundred thousand American that Beaudreau's paying when we get back."

"If we get back," the captain said, shifting the old pipe from one side of his mouth to the other between browned teeth. He was short and muscular, red-haired except for the gray beard streaked by pipe smoke. His eyes were bleary from lack of sleep and from fear. He wore a black pea jacket and a wool skullcap. Strange, he thought, the money didn't seem so important now.

"Beaudreau says they're afraid to start an all-out shooting war. No sweat. We go in and do our thing and get the hell out. That's it," the mate said. He was younger than the captain's forty years; perhaps he'd seen thirty birthdays. He was tall, ungainly, wore his hair in a long pigtail and frequently spit a brown stream at the cuspidor near the wheel.

Their dinghies sped past port and starboard sides, making for the offshore oil platforms a mile away. It was time to hope and speculate. The frogmen on board were old hands. The charges would be laid, the timers set with no hitches. The captain had inspected the platforms with his glasses and found them almost deserted. Perhaps they would get in and out quickly enough.

ON THE HOVERCRAFT, the ship-to-shore squawked to life again.

"Nile. Jessup. They've hit the oil rigs."

"How bad is it, Jessup?" Barrabas asked, grim-faced.

"Bad as it can get. We had about eighty men on each of those rigs, and the oil is spreading out from all four. One hell of a mess."

"Damn!" Barrabas cursed in frustration. "Get a new fix on their ship, Jessup. We've got to catch the bastards."

"How fast will this bucket go, Alex?" he asked.

"I've got her at theoretical limits now, Colonel. I don't know her stress limits."

"Let's find out!"

## 11

The Hovercraft slid over the water like a skater on a glassy millpond. One hundred feet long, she was a monster. Her propeller was thirty feet in diameter, mounted on a streamlined fin towering twenty-five feet above the aft thwarts. Air was pushed through the mammoth blades, creating a constant draft of cold air above decks. At thirty-five feet, the diesel's exhaust funnel towered over the whole ship.

She wasn't beautiful by usual nautical standards. From the distance she looked like a kid's inflated tire tube with a toy boat forced into the middle. On each side, toward the forward wheelhouse, powerful rescue boats were slung on davits, ready to be swung off in an emergency.

The SOBs had thought they'd never get used to the noise, but they had. Nanos had poured on the gas, and they rounded the channel into Bristol Bay at almost sixty knots.

"Get Geoff on the horn, Claude," Barrabas ordered. "We're going to need him soon."

The loudspeaker over their heads squawked into life as Hayes called in the helicopter.

"I'm at St. Mary's, Colonel. Problems," Bishop reported.

"Explain!" Barrabas shouted.

"Been here almost an hour, Colonel. The F-16 is here, but she won't fire up now."

"Did the Air Force crew stick around?"

"Yep. They're trying to get her started."

"Are you being jerked around up there, Bishop?" Barrabas asked. He had been afraid of that. They could only be sure of their equipment and tactics if they had complete control. Jessup and his senator friend might think they were telling the CIA and the military the score, but they couldn't control stalling and contrived fuckups.

"You crawl all over those bastards and get airborne," he ordered. "I'm going to call Jessup to back you up. Got that?"

"Loud and clear, Colonel. What about the chopper? Better than sitting here with my finger up my nose."

"We've got almost another hour for you to make it here in time to help with the chopper. If you can't get the F-16 in the air in less than forty minutes, use the chopper."

The SOBs were in the wheelhouse, dressed in battle gear, prepared for boarding. They had M-16s slung over their shoulders and commando knives on their webbing.

Barrabas didn't want to engage the enemy with just the few rockets he had. The F-16's bombs and rockets could make all the difference.

"Get Jessup on the line," he commanded.

The ship-to-shore crackled again. The fat man's voice came through loud and clear. "Jessup here, Nile. I'll have a new set of pictures in five minutes."

"Never mind that. Those bastards at Eielson are jerking us around. They claim the F-16 at St. Mary's won't start up. They're fucking with this operation, Walker. Put a fire under the bastards."

"Will do," he said. "Wait a minute. The courier is here. I've got new pictures. Give me a few seconds to find what I want."

Jessup was off the air for about five minutes. "The Russian ship is approaching Etolin Strait between Nunivak Island and the mainland," he finally said. "Where are you now?"

"Hold on," Barrabas said.

"How long to intercept, Alex?" he asked the Greek.

"Three hours to intercept. We'll hit them in our own waters south of St. Lawrence Island."

"And if Geoff was to get off in the F-16 in the next hour?"

"We could revise our plan for him, Colonel," Nanos said. "He could make it by helicopter about the same time as us."

"Did you hear that, Walker? I'd like him to get the F-16 airborne. I'll give him a half hour, a little more, then he's got to abandon the F-16 and take the chopper."

"I understand. Good shooting. Over and out."

JESSUP MADE EIELSON BY JET in ten minutes. He plodded up the wooden steps of the base commander's building with the determination of a bulldog and with some of that animal's pugnacious expression. The first floor shook with his weight as the duty sergeant looked up from his desk.

"Who is the base commander?" Jessup demanded.

The sergeant, normally a tyrant in his own small puddle, answered without thinking, "Colonel Bartlett Franks, sir."

"Is he in?" Jessup barked.

The fat man saw the sergeant's eyes slide sideways to a door to his right.

"He's busy right now," the noncom said, his face beginning to redden.

Jessup kept right on going like a bull elephant in full charge. It would take more than the sergeant and his cronies to arrest that mass in motion. Before the military man knew what had happened, the big Texan was through the door and out of his sight.

The colonel sat reading official papers at his desk. He was a small dapper man in tailored uniform, looking official and unassailable.

"What the hell's going on at St. Mary's?" Jessup asked, planting his feet in front of the desk and looking down at the little man.

"Who the hell are you," the colonel asked calmly.

His response disturbed Jessup. The man should have been out of his chair and shouting for his people. But he sat there calmly, asking the obvious.

"You were ordered to offer total cooperation. You call the kind of jerking around at St. Mary's cooperation?"

"We sent the jet. It won't start."

"And why won't it start? Your men have been ordered to hold it at St. Mary's?"

"Type of problem happens all the time. I asked who you were," he repeated.

"I'm a man with clout in Washington you wouldn't believe. It was the Secretary of Defense who cut your orders. Now, let's get the jet in St. Mary's in the air."

"Can't do it. Would you like another from here?" The look on his face told the story. He was condescending to a civilian.

"To take three hours to get there? To suddenly develop engine trouble at St. Mary's, like the first one?"

"Happens. We'll do our best."

"Look, you hidebound bastard! You're standing in the way of a vital life-and-death job," Jessup bawled, standing over him like an avenging monster. "You can't see it, you stupid bastard, but you're also standing in the way of your first star."

"My people in St. Mary's tell me they're doing their best. I can order a replacement from here. That's all I can do," the colonel said, a half smile splitting his face.

Jessup had met the type all too often. The offices and corridors of the Pentagon were filled with them. Half the ones he'd met would have taken the same attitude. The job at hand, even danger to their own citizens, was not as important to them as their niche in the military scheme of things. That, and closing ranks against civilians and mercs.

Jessup turned for the door. "You're fools. Petty, jealous fools. We have to put the country first and your damned jealousy last!" he shouted.

"Do the best we can for you," the colonel said, an almost enigmatic smile on his face.

Jessup left. All the pressure he could bring to bear would be too late.

THE RUSSIAN TRAWLER PLOWED through the Bering Sea at about eighteen knots. Barrabas, Nanos and Hayes could see her on radar about fifty miles to the northwest, heading for Russian waters that were just twenty miles the other side of St. Lawrence Island. O'Toole, Hatton and Billy Two were checking armament. Charlie and the Russian were below decks, confined to the salon.

They knew the battleground now. They would intercept just south of the island.

The ship-to-shore blared out. "I'm airborne, Colonel. The F-16 is history. I'll be there in about an hour and a half." Bishop's voice came through loud and clear.

"I read you. Keep me posted. Out."

The loudspeaker was silent.

Nanos turned to his chief. "What's the plan, Colonel?"

"We go in as fast as we can make it. We can't wait for Geoff," he said.

He turned to Hayes. "Make sure our rocket crews are on the ball, Claude."

"I've got the port side with Billy. O'Toole has the starboard with Lee. We know what to do, Colonel."

Time seemed to stand still as the ships closed. They could see the gap narrowing, minute by minute. The great bulk of St. Lawrence Island was now taking up all the top of the radar screen.

"Swing around and come at them from the northwest, Alex. See if we can turn them as we attack."

They could see the Russian ship on radar, now only ten miles to starboard. They cruised past her, out of rocket range, swung around and came at her, bow to bow.

"What's Bishop's ETA now, Alex?" Barrabas asked.

"A half hour, Colonel."

"Let's go get them, Alex. We'll give them a broadside as we pass to port. When we've made one pass, make a one-eighty so our starboard battery can get a shot at them."

"Right, Colonel," Nanos said, concentrating on his maneuvers.

Barrabas stepped outside to the noise of the huge propellers. He moved down the deck to the port missile installation. "You've got first crack at them, Claude. Give them half your load. We'll swing around and let them have it from our starboard battery."

He moved over to the starboard deck and talked to O'Toole and Hatton, then went back to the port battery and stood with Hayes and Billy Two. They sat on cradles beside the pods, sighting as the Hovercraft came about and headed on her southerly course.

Barrabas balanced against the slight sway of the deck, a pair of 7x50s to his eyes. The Russian ship jumped into his view. The decks were alive with men. The covers had been thrown off rocket launchers. He ran his glasses along the deck and realized he would be firing at steel plating with rockets intended for aircraft. Unless he hit something vital, she wouldn't blow.

He also noted an unmarked helicopter coming in from the northwest.

"Get Bishop for me," he commanded.

"Geoff. Where the hell are you?" he asked when he had the connection. "We've got a bogey with no markings, came in from the northwest."

"I'm still twenty minutes away—maybe a little less. What does she look like?" Bishop asked.

"Thin fuselage with two men, one sitting above the other; twin jet engines; high structure for tail fin and rear prop; two stubby wings fore and aft—looks like they've replaced armament with long-distance pods, four of them," Barrabas recited.

"Italian," Bishop said. "Can also be refueled in the air. Think it's a spotter, Colonel?"

"Could be." He trained his glasses on the sleek aircraft. "Can't see a single gun or missile. Can't be anything but a spotter."

"Could be the Russians looking over the action. Bet my share there isn't a Russian on the trawler," Nanos offered without taking his eyes from the other ship. "They're keeping an eye on the hired help."

"Okay, Geoff. See you soon. We're going in now," Barrabas concluded.

The two ships approached with a combined closing speed of more than sixty knots, rapidly gaining on each other. The shots would have to be right on.

"Aim for the deck crews," Barrabas shouted over the sound of wind and propellers.

As they flashed past, Hayes and Billy Two fired five of their rockets. Tails of blue and red flame blew out of the tubes, and five trails of fire flared toward the steel-hulled ship.

Two Russian rockets streaked at the Hovercraft, both high, barely missing the funnel. The Russian ship passed astern and Barrabas saw that three of the rockets had exploded on their decks, taking out one rocket crew and damaging the wheelhouse.

Nanos turned her 180 degrees in a few seconds, and they rushed through the waves at fifty knots again.

Barrabas scrambled to the starboard side. O'Toole and Hatton were ready, eyes pressed to sights.

Again they came up on the trawler. Five missiles flashed away, their fiery trails arcing toward the old ship.

The enemy sent three missiles screaming across the water, this time lower. One passed astern, one hit the funnel and blew it away, and the third hit the landing ramp forward, blowing the front off the salon. Debris drifted upward, smashing the roof off the wheelhouse.

O'Toole and Hatton's shots had missed, except for one rocket that had taken down the Russian's forward superstructure.

As Barrabas ran to the wheelhouse, Nanos was bringing her around again.

"We've lost about five to eight knots, Colonel," Nanos screamed over the noise of the propeller. "Where did we take hits?" The Greek stood at the wheel, with blood streaming from small cuts on his face.

"No critical hits. We lost the stack and the front of the salon. You all right, Alex?"

"Just cuts, Colonel. What about Charlie and the Russian? They were right where we took a direct hit."

"No time to find out. Let's take another run. Same as the first, but on their starboard side."

THE RED-HAIRED FRENCH SKIPPER of the trawler relinquished the wheel and moved as though he was in a trance to assess his damage. He hadn't bargained for this. Beaudreau had said it was in and out. A piece of cake. Where the hell did the enemy get a Hovercraft from in these waters? Damned thing could sail circles around them.

The first mate sat against the forward rocket launchers, holding a rag to his head. His whole pea jacket was a mass of blood. The rocket crew was dead, their mangled bodies spread around the deck in puddles of blood.

"Get us the hell out of here, Skipper," the first mate wailed. "That damned floating balloon's going to sink us."

"I'm keeping her at full revs. Who's in the helicopter? Theirs or ours?" the captain asked.

"Damned if I know," the first mate complained. "Wouldn't put it past the damned Russians to just sit up there and watch."

The thought chilled the captain to the bone. He didn't like it. The Russians didn't jeopardize their own lives just to watch.

THE BIG HOVERCRAFT CIRCLED gracefully, riding the water as if by magic. The steel trawler lumbered like a wounded old bear heading for the safety of her den, in this case Russian waters.

As they approached once more, O'Toole and Hatton had first crack. Their last five rockets blasted away. Five streams of fire raced toward the trawler.

Through the 7x50s, Barrabas could see direct hits on the deck, and bodies went flying. One rocket hit the steel plating of the hull and curled it. Two rockets whistled harmlessly overhead.

Barrabas spent the next few minutes racing between the missile emplacements and the wheelhouse. If they couldn't take out the trawler on the next pass, they would go in and strafe with the 50 mm until Bishop showed up.

By the time he had delivered his orders and placed himself next to Hayes and Billy, the big machine was racing on course for their last missile shots.

Again the blast of five rockets torc at his ears. He traced their paths in his field glasses.

They made five hits from stem to stern. The deck of the trawler exploded in fire and shards of steel. As Barrabas took the glasses from his eyes and raised his hand in a salute to his gunners, an explosion rocked the Hovercraft. The propeller, along with its mount, was blasted clear off its aft position, and the ship wallowed in her own wash.

"Hayes!" Barrabas screamed over the noise of the flotation fans. "Get the boats lowered and our people aboard. I'm going below!"

He raced to the wreckage of the salon. The front companionway had been blown away with the landing ramp that had covered it. The salon was open to the sky. The smell of cordite and burned rocket fuel filled the air. A fire had started aft near the fuel tanks.

He saw no one.

Wreckage had been blown into the large room that had been the crew's dining and recreation area. Barrabas searched as quickly as he could. He could still hear the props that kept them afloat creating a cushion of air, but they were within Russian rocket range and could be blown out of the water at any moment. The fire could do the same.

"Charlie!" he screamed. "Where the hell are you?"

"Colonel? We're under the table." The sound was muffled, the voice unsteady.

A dining table, blown off its retaining clamps, was under a pile of rubble. Barrabas put both hands under a ledge and exerted all his strength. He strained from above while the two Eskimos pushed from below. Slowly the table and the rubble moved, and the two men crawled out. Barrabas let go, and the mass of wreckage fell to the deck.

"Are you both okay?" he asked.

"We're all right, Colonel," Charlie answered for both of them.

He could hear the diesel start to sputter and fail. The fans started to slow. "Let's get the hell out of here," he said, leading the way.

Above decks, the odor of cordite and rocket fuel had blown off. About two miles away, the trawler was trailing smoke but making way at about five or six knots.

One of the SOB rescue boats was standing clear with Hayes at the control. He had O'Toole, Hatton and Billy Two with him.

Nanos had pulled the second boat alongside and had a ladder strung for them to climb down. As Barrabas helped the Eskimos down the ladder, two rockets screamed overhead. He jumped into the boat after them, and Nanos gave her full power.

"Radio in the panel in front of you, Colonel. It's tuned to Bishop's channel," Nanos said.

"Come in, Bishop. Come in, Bishop."

"Loud and clear, Colonel," Bishop responded. "I see smoke on the horizon. What's going down?"

"The smoke is from the trawler, but we haven't stopped her. She's crippled, but still making way. Do you have the firepower to take her down?"

"Maybe, Colonel. It's questionable. With a direct hit on her ammunition hold—maybe. What about you people?"

"Abandoned ship. We're all okay, but in the rescue boats. We're heading for St. Lawrence Island. When you're finished, pick us up at Southeast Cape on the tip of the island."

"Will do, Colonel. Over and out."

As they tuned out, the two rescue craft cleared the Hovercraft by a half mile. Barrabas turned to take a last look when a rocket from the trawler hit her amidships. The fuel tank blew. A huge cloud of red flame curled upward, surrounded by black smoke.

An acrid cloud that smelled of burned wood and rubber drifted across the water with the prevailing wind. The sea was relatively calm as they raced toward the large island to the northeast.

BISHOP TURNED the streamlined Bell helicopter in for his first run. Beck was at the console of the arming and tracking computers, making sure their radar-directed missile strikes were on target.

The high-caliber machine guns opened up on the deck of the trawler as Bishop zoomed in. His speed was more than two hundred miles an hour, but compared to the attack capability of an F-16, he seemed to hang in the sky.

On his first pass, Bishop unleashed two rockets from a range of about a mile. He followed them in, dropping two HE bombs from pods under the cockpit.

The mystery helicopter made no move to take part in the battle.

Bishop's rockets hit the deck of the trawler, taking out most of the crew who were still on their feet. The two bombs came in low, skipped across the steel deck plating without detonating and splashed into the sea.

As he turned for a second run, the ship erupted in a huge ball of orange flame from bow to stern.

Bishop had to turn hard to port in an evasive maneuver to avoid the massive updraft from the explosion.

The trawler broke in two. The bow and the stern, in different locations, pointed toward the sky. Then the weight of steel overcame the buoyancy of gases still trapped in the hull, and both sections disappeared in seconds.

It hadn't been Bishop's bomb that had dealt the fatal blow. As they watched, the mystery Russian helicopter disappeared toward the Russian coast.

"LET'S SEE if they have survivors," Barrabas said, watching through the binoculars.

Nanos put on full revs and turned in a quick ninety-degree arc toward the boat. Hayes followed, his warriors at the thwarts, their M-16s cocked and ready.

Nanos made several passes through the wreckage floating on the oily waters. They saw no one. Slowly he brought her around and pointed the bow toward St. Lawrence Island, the second rescue boat keeping as close as possible.

Bishop flew over, wagged the rotor left to right and headed for the island.

"What now, Colonel?" Nanos asked over the sound of the motor.

We'll report to Jessup and have him equip us for a strike at the National Petroleum Reserve research station on the North Slope two days from now."

"What do you think about the trawler going down, Colonel?" Nanos asked. "Didn't look like any sinking I've ever seen."

"I agree," Barrabas said. "You got any thoughts?"

In the other boat, Liam O'Toole, the SOBs demolitions expert, had been listening over the intercom. He broke in.

"I hate to think anyone, even the Russians, are so damned low, Colonel, but I'd swear the ship was blown by the chopper." He paused to look his chief in the eye across the water separating them. "They weren't there to observe. Their job was to destroy all evidence."

## 12

The Bell 222 stood silent, her skids resting on a shelf of rock. To the local people, silhouetted against the slowly darkening sky, she looked like some kind of prehistoric monster.

The rebuilding of Deadhorse had progressed miraculously in the past few days. The men who had been sent to replace the dead felt the need for shelter against future attacks and were fighting time. The terminal of the Alaska Pipeline was still intact.

The SOBs were relaxing in Charlie Dayo's house. They had all met Chank's extended family, and now they were alone with Charlie and their Yupik prisoner.

"Still looks fishy as hell to me, Colonel," Nanos was saying. "That old tub didn't blow like you'd expect. Wasn't Beck's bombs and it wasn't the magazine. Damned thing exploded from stem to stern all at once. Someone had her prewired to blow."

"Looked that way to me, too," Barrabas said. "The trawler was manned by hired hands, and the Russians pulled the plug. A cover-up." He paused and looked around at the group. "We've got to forget the last battle. We've got a decision to make. I'm not totally convinced the coming raid we've been told about is genuine," Barrabas was saying. "Why would they let one of their Yupik warriors know their plans in advance."

"I went over it carefully with him, Colonel," Charlie said. "He's not changing his story."

"I'm not expecting him to. But maybe they informed their Yupik recruits so it would be passsed on to us," Barrabas said.

"That would be one hell of a long shot, Colonel," O'Toole said. "They would have to lose Yupiks as captives, and the Yupiks would have to talk. Odds are just too long."

"Suppose you're right and our prisoner is telling the truth. Next question is, why would they continue on the north shore after two failures in a row?" Barrabas asked, looking around at the group.

Lee Hatton knew the colonel was probing all the possibilities before they went into action the next day. Jessup had arranged for weapons and battle dress to be flown in for them. They'd have everything to do the job. Barrabas's questions were designed to get a consensus on whether they had a battle to fight the next day or not.

There was a knock on the cabin door. Charlie got up from his place by the fire and answered it. A tall blond man gave Charlie a written message and left. Charlie handed it to their leader.

Barrabas took a minute to read and digest the note before he looked up.

"From Jessup," he said. "He's been keeping track of the Russian activity at their Chukchi base. The other fake Greenpeace ship left port yesterday, and now it's off Cape Lisburne, heading for Point Barrow. He figures it's about eighteen hours from the research center."

He looked around the group. "Not much doubt now. They'll be in a position to attack in eighteen to twenty hours. I want to be there at least two hours before them. If they have radar, they will pick us up unless we come in very low." He pulled a pack of stogies from a pocket and fired one as he looked at the nine weary faces. "I suggest we all get a good sleep and be up at dawn."

As he finished, the door crashed open, and a woman stooped to walk through. She seemed surprised to see so many people, but not surprised enough to stop at the door. She spotted Nanos.

"I heard you were back," she said, her voice the roar of a hundred-mile-an-hour wind.

"Kaweetha!" Nanos said weakly, looking up at her towering form in surprise. He looked at his friends, as if in supplication.

The big woman bent and picked up the weight lifter with ease, hoisted him across her shoulder and headed out of the room.

"Good night, Alex," Billy Two called after them.

Lee looked around the group and smiled. The entry of the big woman was just what they needed. They were smiling as they broke up to go to their assigned sleeping quarters.

Bishop caught her eye. They exchanged a silent message, then shrugged, each resigned to a night alone.

IN THE LUXURIOUS APARTMENT of the first secretary, the lights shone well into the night. The man was a terror for work. Sleeping only four hours a night, usually from four to eight, he kept his staff busy the other twenty hours.

A door opened in the small den where he sat, and one of his aides showed in the director of the First Chief Directorate of the KGB.

Mesmerof looked exhausted. He also had a wary expression, and that was something the first secretary had never noted before. It wasn't good for one of his top men to show fear. Probably the time had come for Mesmerof to retire to his dacha on the Black Sea. The general didn't look good at all. Although fat as ever, he seemed to float around in his suit, which hung on him like an old sack. New folds of flesh had formed under his eyes, emphasizing his look of exhaustion. His skin had taken on a sickly pallor.

"Sit, General. Will you have a drink?" the first secretary offered, as though moved by sympathy to relax his stand against alcohol.

"Thank you. Not just now."

The first time he'd ever seen Mesmerof refuse a drink, the first secretary thought. Not at all the man's usual style, according to rumor. It had to be worry about the Greenpeace job. Bad. Very bad. The man had handled hundreds of jobs more dangerous. Mesmerof actually seemed to think that the Americans would push the button because they'd lost a few oil rigs.

"I thought the last raid went well," the Soviet leader said as Mesmerof sat uncomfortably in front of him.

"We were lucky. If the ship hadn't been wired..."

"The Americans would have blown it. Or whoever was in the helicopter."

"You knew about that?" Mesmerof asked.

The first secretary didn't feel obliged to answer the obvious. "I said it would work. If our people do a job on the experimental station, it'll be over. We'll have won."

"I wish you'd let us cancel it. The Americans know we're behind it. The whole world's got to know by now. I don't like it."

"Maybe." The first secretary smiled, pleased with himself. "But they can't pin it on us. That's the important thing. By now, they have to feel the French are involved."

"I wish I had your confidence," Mesmerof said, his voice low and without its usual strength.

"And why not? I fed them a pawn to question. By this time, they know about Beaudreau and his payoff."

"You sent—they have someone...?" Mesmerof's voice trailed off.

"Something that should have been done by your people. I also got to the American military. A little interservice rivalry never hurts. Slowed things down a bit."

"Yes, First Secretary," Mesmerof answered, as if by rote. He was stunned. His Directorate had blown it. The first secretary had been ahead of him every step of the way.

"What's your impression of the group they sent after your raiders?"

"The group? They seem very professional."

"Tells us a great deal. Not military. Nothing official. Insignia all painted out."

"How did you know—"

"It's as I told you. They aren't sure who's behind it and don't want to take the chance of a major conflict."

"Yes, First Secretary."

"Now, listen carefully, General. I don't want any slipups here." The most powerful man in the USSR leaned forward in his overstuffed chair. He clipped the end off a cigar and threw the bit of tobacco into the fireplace. "Make sure Beaudreau is aboard the trawler for this last show, along with the last of his cronies. We don't want any loose ends. Petrov did a beautiful job pulling the plug in the Bering Sea, and I'm counting on him to repeat the performance."

"Yes, First Secretary," Mesmerof said, almost mesmerized by the plot that was becoming too much for him.

"And, General. We shouldn't have to remind a professional like Petrov, but just in case something goes wrong, tell him to clean out his pockets."

"Yes, First Secretary," Mesmerof said. He was beyond rational thought and retreated inside himself, almost into a comatose state. Still able to move, he pulled himself erect, turned and left the room without another word.

The first secretary made a mental note to relieve Mesmerof from his post. Maybe someone else should talk to Petrov. But no, the Soviet leader corrected himself. Petrov was a professional who would know what to do.

IN A DEFILE between outcrops in the Arctic tundra, Barrabas and his soldiers unloaded the crates sent up from Eielson's stores. They had black fatigues, body armor, a half dozen of the new M-16A2s in the 733 Commando Model and a half dozen in the 40 mm grenade launcher Model 203. One CAW, a Close Assault Weapon, which was an automatic 12-gauge shotgun, was quickly grabbed by Billy.

One of the carefully packed boxes contained two AN/PVS-4 night sights and two sonic distant sound detectors. Despite other military foul-ups, whoever sent their supplies was on the ball. More than enough ammunition had been included for the M-16A2s in

Mag-Pac format, a box of a hundred grenades, three one-hundred-watt walkie-talkies and a box of commando knives with sheaths.

Bishop's chopper stood close by. He and Beck were adapting the mountings of a half dozen Penguin radar-controlled antiship missiles to the underside of her belly, and a couple of 50 mm cannon on the ends of her stunted forward planes.

As they pulled on fatigues and armor, blackened their faces and fastened on webbing, the first sign of the enemy appeared on the horizon a few miles out.

"She'll be at least an hour at full speed before she's close enough to discharge assault troops," Nanos offered.

Barrabas turned to Bishop, who had just finished the missile installation. "Let's get the bird up and have a look, Geoff," he said.

"You want to give away our presence?" Bishop asked.

"Better we know what we're up against than maintain complete secrecy," Barrabas said.

He turned to Beck. "How's the infrared sensor display on the 222, Nate?" he asked. "Can you give us a count of the personnel on board?"

"State of the art, Colonel. Should be able to give you an almost exact count. Depends what kind of shields they have, if any."

"Okay. You two get airborne and report back as soon as possible."

When they had gone, Barrabas turned to the others. He waited until the bird was airborne and her prop noise abated.

"Two groups," he said. "O'Toole takes Hayes and Nanos. Billy and Lee will be with me. Everyone should have a grenade launcher. I want the best antipersonnel barrage possible laid down when they wade ashore."

"How about the night sights and the sound detectors?" O'Toole asked.

"One of each for you and me, Liam. I'm taking a second M-16A2. You'd better do the same," Barrabas said. "Nanos and Hatton carry the radios. Billy will have the CAW for close work. Any questions?"

As he asked the question, Hatton was picking up one of the radios tuned to Bishop's frequency. It squawked a message. She held it to her ear and asked for a repeat.

"Bad news, Colonel," she said. "Close to thirty men on the ship, give or take two or three, and something else. Very strange."

"Spit it out, Lee."

"Twenty other bodies on Nate's sensors. They're ashore, behind us, a hundred yards and closing."

"Right. We split into two groups. We'll saturate the area with grenades, then take them in a cross fire. Move!"

The two groups moved silently to a position twenty yards to left and right of where they had been, but facing inshore.

Barrabas looked through his night sight. "Listen up," he whispered into the mike. "Enemy fifty yards straight ahead. Fire on the count of three. Go!"

Six grenades flew from six M-16A2s and exploded amid enemy ranks. Smoke and screams filled the night as the last of the light disappeared for some. The mercs couldn't see the carnage, but they knew they'd taken out a few of the enemy.

The SOBs followed Barrabas's lead and fired another round, then charged, their commando knives slung loose in sheaths. Five or six small-statured men advanced through the smell of cordite that was blown toward the SOBs by an offshore breeze.

Billy fired the CAW three shells at a time, working the pump and trigger with lightning speed. Three men burst apart and were spread around on the rocks, their uniforms shredded, their flesh a part of the landscape. One stocky form rushed Hatton with his bayonet.

"Look out!" Hayes shouted from her left.

As the man lunged, he pulled the trigger of his AK and caught Hatton in the chest. She went down. Barrabas's knife sliced through flesh between the attacker's ribs and carved a hole in his heart.

"Lee! You all right?" Barrabas asked.

She was curled up, holding her chest. The round must have punched against the bulletproof padding like the hoof of a mule. "I'll live," she said. "Don't stop for me."

Nanos cut loose with his M-16 and took out two of the men with short bursts. As the bullets hit flesh, their bodies, torn and lifeless, hurtled back at their milling comrades.

The enemy regrouped and pushed on, still firing.

O'Toole found himself facing a foe at a distance of twenty feet and fired. The man went down in a hail of steel, one of his rounds slicing the side of O'Toole's thigh.

The last man came charging like a tiger, a snarl on his lips. He thrust out his rifle trying to skewer Barrabas. Hayes took him under the armpit with his knife, lifting him off his feet. Blood spewed.

Barrabas, Nanos, Hayes and Billy Two surveyed the landscape. They saw no one standing.

"Claude, I'm going to check on our wounded. Take the others and check out the dead," Barrabas commanded. "We don't want any of those bastards at our back when the others come ashore."

They disappeared through the pall of smoke. He bent to Hatton and pulled her to a sitting position. Her armor had been beaten up badly, but the round hadn't penetrated. She'd have a hell of a bruise for a while.

"Are you okay, Lee?" he asked.

She grimaced. "I'll live. God almighty, that was one hell of a punch!"

"Liam's down. See to him while I check out the field. We've got to get the hell out of here and down to the beach."

He took off at a trot, thankful they had not fared worse. Without the warning from Beck, they could have been dead meat.

But they had been damned lucky. If Barrabas hadn't ordered the chopper up, they would have been caught in a pincer while fighting the men coming ashore. It was all part of the soldiering—counting on luck. That wasn't enough, though. What counted was the kind of group they had, and the individuals who added their determination and skills. If they hadn't been professionals, they would have bought it with that particular battle.

**13**

On the Russian trawler, just outside the wheelhouse, Beaudreau put the rubber cushions of the 10x35 glasses to his eyes and focused carefully. The last of the daylight and the roll of the ship made it difficult to be sure of what he saw.

The glasses were good, although not as good as his old World War II German 7x50s at home. He counted six mercenaries. He wondered if it was possible there was only the six of them plus the ones who were acting as their eye in the sky. Maybe they had suffered casualties in the other battles, and with their ranks depleted, wouldn't put up a strong show. They were outnumbered six to one.

Before the last light faded, Beaudreau had managed to pick out some details. The enemy troops were clad in black fatigues and faced away from the shore, but he caught a glimpse of red hair from beneath the knitted cap of one tall man. A tuft of white was momentarily visible under the cap of another.

A tall man with black hands took up his field of vision. Could be combat cosmetics, Beaudreau thought, then considered it unlikely.

The tallest of the group was the next one he tried to focus on. A very tall man indeed. The fifth was broad-shouldered and seemed to have a more stocky build.

The sixth mercenary held Beaudreau's interest. Shorter than the others, the merc's body seemed less bulkier, too. At first Beaudreau thought the merc was a native, like the men he was using, except for the way the bottom of the fatigues were filled out. Nice and full, as if it was the behind of a woman.

A woman? Couldn't be.

As he watched, he was aware that he should be more concerned about his strategy and the men he had dropped off earlier and who were being mowed down by the mercs. But the one with the rear end like a woman's fascinated him. Must be female, he decided.

Suddenly Beaudreau noticed one of his men charging at her, bayonets at the ready.

*"Regardez!"* Beaudreau mouthed soundlessly. "Look out!"

As the words were formed by his lips, she went down, apparently taking a direct shot to her chest.

It was all too close and real. Beaudreau hadn't thought about blood and death when he'd taken the money. He had felt afraid for the past couple of days. Afraid for his own skin. No word had reached him from the other trawler and the crew he'd hired. The last word he'd heard was of a sea battle and the trawler limping home. The one question mark in his mind revolved around an unidentified chopper that had trailed his other ship like an observer. Who had piloted it? Was it Russian or American?

He was glad that everything would be over soon. Just as that thought had entered his mind, an armed chopper dove over the trawler without firing. He followed its flight and lost it in the distance. Then, far out at sea, his glasses picked up an unmarked chopper. He scanned it closely. It wasn't armed. Instead of armaments, it was equipped with long-distance pods. That meant only one thing. It had to be the unidentified chopper—the observer.

COLONEL PETROV WATCHED the battle from the observer's seat in the Italian A129 Mangusta. He'd seen the American mercs take on the advance force and, against all odds, take them out to the man. He didn't like the setup. The Bell 222 had taken off again and was capable of sinking the trawler. It was also capable of taking him out with one rocket.

"Keep well clear of the action," he ordered the pilot. "Remember, we're here to observe. And we have to get back to report."

He remembered the last time he'd seen Mesmerof. The man was starting to disintegrate before his eyes. The thought sustained him as he watched the troops leave the trawler for shore. No matter what happened here, he would soon be the director of the most powerful of the KGB's directorates.

The thought pumped the adrenaline. He swelled with pride. It was the goal he'd set for himself for years, and it was only days away.

NATE BECK SAT BEHIND a battery of CRT monitors, in his own kind of heaven. The noise of the rotors above his head was surprisingly low. He could hear himself hum contentedly through his earphones as he went about his work.

He had a front row seat to the firefight below. It came at him in flashes of orange light as the grenades exploded and in a semaphore of light when the small-arms fire sped across the tundra.

He palmed a Talk switch on his chest. "Is Lee all right, Colonel?" he asked.

"She'll have a bruise, nothing more."

"You want us to take out the ship now, Colonel?" Bishop had told him to act as his ears on this one while he looked after the flying and watched the monitors for birds coming at them from the ship.

The answer was lost to him as Bishop called out, "Bird coming in at three o'clock!"

Beck didn't have to look out at three o'clock to see it. He saw it on his monitor and read off the diminishing range. While Bishop banked sharply to port, Beck loosed a sunburst that was picked up by the missile's sensors and did its job as a decoy.

"What was your answer, Colonel?" Beck asked casually. He didn't worry about incoming missiles. He had the only philosophy he could handle with this job—the one about a round having your number on it, and no sense worrying in the meantime.

"Not yet, Nate. When their landing force disembarks, let them get close in before you attack. We don't want the mother ship worrying about us. You keep her busy."

"Can do, Colonel," Beck said, closing off the circuit.

He began to hum again and swung his gaze back and forth across his monitors.

BARRABAS FELT A LOT BETTER about the situation than he had fifteen minutes earlier. His people were now deployed. Through the powerful lens of his AN/PVS-4, he saw six boatloads of troops leave the Greenpeace ship and head inshore.

Six boats, and up to four men to a boat. Twenty-four was the maximum, he thought. He assumed the minimum could be half that.

He talked into his radio. "Liam. Grenades. We'll arc them in high and try for fragmentation over their heads."

"I read you," the big redhead answered.

Barrabas loaded his grenade launcher, pointed the M-16A2 skyward and squeezed the forward trigger. The others followed his lead. The noise and smoke surrounded them as Barrabas strained through his night sight to see the effect of the barrage.

He couldn't see any damage.

"Let's give them two more rounds, Liam," he shouted into his mike.

"Right, Colonel."

As the SOBs lobbed grenades through the air, Barrabas watched through his optics. The fragmentation was too spread out, and the enemy was taking hits with few casualties. He swung the glass toward the ship. Four more boats had been launched.

"Bishop. Come in, Bishop."

"This is Beck, Colonel. Geoff's busy."

"Did I see you adapting a multiwarhead fragmentation bomb to the 222?"

"They shipped only one, Colonel. Notice the second wave of boats launched from Big Momma?"

"They are your target, Nate. Take them all out, if you can. Over and out."

The first wave of boats was closer now, well within SOB range.

"Forget the grenades!" Barrabas yelled into the mike. "Take out this first wave with small-arms fire. Bishop is taking out the second wave."

He held his fire, waiting for a shot with maximum effect.

The boats were at the apex of a triangle now, with O'Toole's crew at one end of the base and his at the other.

Before opening fire, he thumbed his radio. "You all right, Liam? How's the thigh?" he asked.

"Your timing's lousy, Colonel. I'm okay, but I'm a wee bit busy right now."

Barrabas smiled to himself as he loosed his first burst at the incoming boats. A mortar whistled past his head and exploded twenty yards behind. He opened fire.

His rounds scythed the flesh off the men in the lead boat. His people were full-bent into battle, churning up the water around the boats with lethal rounds and taking out many of the invaders before they could return effective fire. Fresh winds from the sea carried the smell of cordite away from them.

To his left, Barrabas saw a rocket streak off toward the ship. The Bell 222 circled to make a pass at the second wave of boats.

BISHOP WAS ENJOYING HIMSELF. With Beck in the seat behind him, he could safely concentrate on the ship while Barrabas was under fire. He turned into the wind to come at the ship on her starboard side from the land. Should he overshoot, he'd rather have the missile drift off to sea.

"Arm number one," he called to Beck on the intercom.

"Roger. Armed."

He flicked his aiming visor down, centered the viewer amidships and fired.

He couldn't see the whole trajectory of the rocket but knew Beck would be guiding it down by radar. As he came about, Beck yelled into the intercom, "Bingo!"

At long range, wheeling around for a shot at the small boats, Bishop saw a plume of smoke from the ship and the flash of a rocket launching. He called out the location to Beck.

The rocket lunged straight toward them.

"Port, skipper! Hard to port!" Beck called.

Bishop moved the control smoothly. As he eased to the left, Beck loosed a sunburst straight down the missile's gullet, making it blow not far from the chopper.

They were rocked by the backlash and debris. Bishop felt pain in an ankle, and blood trickled down his shin.

He turned again, bent on another attack. "Arm number two," he barked.

"What about the colonel's order?"

"Right. This one is all yours, Nate. What altitude you want?"

"Make it two thousand feet. Put me on line and forget it. Keep an eye on the ship. Don't want my pants singed while we're locking on."

Bishop turned fifty degrees to port and climbed to two thousand. He set a course that would take them parallel to the shoreline and then concentrated on the ship.

Within twenty seconds, he felt the slight lurch as they lost the weight of the bomb. He circled to watch the effect as Nate shouted, "Bomb away!"

The silver cylinder floated down, her fins keeping her on target.

At just over fifty feet, an explosion multiplied the bomb into a hundred smaller missiles that blanked the sea in a hundred-yard radius. They blew at about twenty feet. The sea round the boats churned into a froth as thousands of steel shards rained downward.

Bishop descended slowly to fifty feet to view the carnage. All the boats had been shredded. Bodies hung over the punctured thwarts. As he watched, the outboard motors pulled the deflating boats to the bottom, leaving a dozen corpses floating on the surface.

Neither man spoke. It gave them no pleasure to see death so quick and horrible. One minute the invaders had been men eager for battle, the next they were strips of flesh and shards of bone.

"Did you see the enemy chopper?" Beck asked Bishop. "It's been on my radar for the past two minutes."

"I saw it. Same as the one down south."

"I'll call the colonel," Beck said. "It's not dangerous to him yet, but he may want it taken down."

O'TOOLE WAS STRETCHED FULL-LENGTH on the hard pebbles of the beach, the sling of his M-16 Commando Model wrapped around his right arm. As he squeezed off short bursts, the pain in his thigh chewed away at him. Lee had wrapped it in a pressure bandage and given him a shot of morphine.

A mortar landed too close, spraying him with pebbles. One hit him in the temple and stunned him for a moment.

"Those bastards might get lucky," he called to Nanos and Hayes. "Full auto. Blast the bastards!"

He forgot about the pain as he clicked over to full auto and held the bucking weapon steady. The boats were close. They had taken a hell of a pounding. He could hear shotgun blasts to his left as Billy switched over to the 12-gauge CAW.

For the next few minutes, all he could hear was the insistent chatter of small-arms fire and the booming of the 12-gauge.

While he was maintaining a steady hail of lead, a flash of fire streaked through the darkened sky.

A few seconds later an explosion above the second wave of boats commanded his attention. The multiple warheads from the chopper blew all at once.

A hail of steel shards raced down to catch the Russians in hell.

BEAUDREAU DUCKED under a metal chart table as the helicopter headed in and fired its second missile. The streak of flame was fast, with only seconds between the time he lost sight of the aircraft and the shudder of the ship when the missile hit.

That made two hits. Beaudreau eased himself from under the table and looked around. The crew of the ship stood by their posts. He was scared. This was not his normal duty. If the damned American pilot got lucky, they could be blown out of the water, and it would all be over.

While he was thinking about his own hide, an explosion flashed before his eyes, not two hundred yards to port. He had hardly regained normal vision when hundreds of small explosions filled the air. A rain of steel descended on the men in the inflatables like the wrath of Thor. The water churned around them and their boats sank.

He looked at the sight openmouthed, then screamed at the captain. "Set a course for home! Get the hell out of here!"

"What about the others?" the captain asked calmly.

"Expendable. Get the hell out of here! Now!"

BARRABAS STOPPED FIRING and looked at the sight before him. It was a scene from hell. Smoke from the small arms and mortars drifted in the offshore breeze.

The first wave of boats had stopped their forward motion. Men hung from the rubber thwarts, their blood streaming into the water. Almost all were dead.

"Cease fire!" he called to Hatton and Billy Two on his right.

He thumbed the radio. "Liam. Come in, Liam."

"Colonel. Think they've had it?"

"Cease fire. Let's look them over. Be careful we don't have some playing possum," he ordered.

The boats were tossed toward shore on two-foot waves. Nothing moved. The mother ship had turned tail and left her brood, with Bishop still in pursuit.

The merc leader cautiously walked to his left, in the direction of O'Toole and his group. Hatton and Billy

Two followed. He could see the other three SOBs moving casually toward him as the boats, now about to beach, drifted between his two groups.

. Three boats left. The other three had taken too many slugs and had sunk. Bodies, singly and in groups, floated nearby.

Barrabas held up a hand and sank to the ground. He waited.

He stood and moved to the boats, now beached by the insistent waves. The water at his feet was stained pink with blood. Four or five bodies had been washed ashore by the waves.

"Check everyone carefully," he ordered as the six SOBs met up.

"One over here will make it," Doc Lee called out from the boat farthest from Barrabas.

"One here still breathing, Colonel," Hayes called from another boat.

"Get the survivors on the beach," he ordered.

He looked out to sea. The fake *Rainbow Warrior* had made some progress, but was streaming smoke. He saw Bishop launch another rocket and watched the burst of flame as it engulfed a part of the ship.

Beck called to him on the radio. "Colonel. The other chopper is up here observing. What do you want me to do?"

"I think he blew the other trawler. I'd like to capture this one," Barrabas said. "Tell Bishop to shoot it down. Then turn the trawler back to us."

Suddenly an explosion rocked the shoreline, and the trawler lurched in the water, mortally wounded. She had blown at a dozen places and was sinking fast.

"The Russian chopper!" Barrabas cried. "Get him, Nate!" he screamed into his microphone. "No matter what you have to do, get him!"

BISHOP TURNED IN PURSUIT of the Italian-made helicopter. Within minutes, he was coming at her head-on.

The chopper turned, taking evasive action. She headed for shore and dropped to a few feet above the sea.

"Arm five and six!" Bishop ordered.

"Armed!"

Bishop pushed the firing button, and Beck guided the rocket on its deadly path.

The A129 was hit in the tail. She yawed left, then right, and hit the water at 150 miles an hour. The light chop that had been disturbed by the plunging whirlybird was back to normal in seconds. The machine had gone to the bottom.

BARRABAS WATCHED THE KILL, straight in front of him, a half mile out. He thumbed the Talk button again. "Nice shooting, Nate. Get a patch from Eielson to Washington and call the CIA number. We need some bag men up here."

As he disconnected, he looked at the spot where the Russian chopper had gone down. He triangulated from two points along the shoreline and mentally made a note of the spot.

## 14

Charlie Dayo's cabin was unique to the town. Almost two hundred miles north of wooded country, a cabin that was made of foot-thick logs had to be totally different. A trader, determined to have the warmest house in Deadhorse, had hauled in the logs and hired Eskimo labor to build it more than a century earlier.

The building next door, the community center, was different in every way. It had been built of inch-thick lapboard and had been used for years without being insulated. During those years the people had complained of the cold while they sat on rough benches at meetings. Now it was warmer, insulated inside. The interior walls of wood veneer made it look finished, if somewhat barren.

In the one big room, Beck had lit a fire in the pot-bellied stove to ward off the bone-chilling cold of Arctic spring. Billy had set up two collapsible tables nearby, and they had laid out the wounded Yupik fighters for Doc Lee's ministrations.

As she clipped off their uniforms with surgical scissors, Lee gave them reassuring nods and encouraging looks.

"It's all right. We will not hurt you," she said, hoping they'd understand from her tone. "We know you had to do what you were told."

Her hands were gentle as she peeled cloth from open wounds. She could see that the men were grateful for her careful treatment.

One man had two slugs through his left shoulder. The exit wounds had torn away flesh and bone, leaving a ragged hole filled with bone splinters. The other had three leg wounds, all penetrating muscle without bone damage. Both men had suffered loss of blood, a good deal, and were still slightly sedated from the shots she had given them on the beach. She would sedate them further, but not until they had been able to communicate with Charlie.

For fifteen minutes, she worked with care, watched as Charlie interrogated them. Finally, after their wounds had been cleaned and covered with surgical dressings, she gave them each a shot of morphine.

Barrabas wandered over, his face a mask of neutrality.

"Have you learned anything?" he asked Charlie.

"Not much. They were in the same briefing sessions as Josef Garin. They know of no other raids. They have no idea who ordered the raids or why. Like Garin, they were trained by Russians, and they saw some others from time to time. They think they were European."

"I didn't think they would know much," Barrabas said. "Tell them we will not harm them. They will be shipped home or they can stay in America."

As they talked, Geoff Bishop wandered over.

"Only one way I know of to get what we want," Barrabas said.

"Exactly what is that, Colonel?" Bishop asked.

"Capture their commander or someone who knows the whole story," Barrabas said.

"We need more intelligence," Bishop said.

"We may not get permission," Barrabas offered. "This is one hell of a sensitive area. I'll call Jessup. Let him get through the red tape. In the meantime, we all relax."

AT THE ALASKA INN, Jessup was preparing for bed. He had just ordered a couple of western sandwiches and a pot of coffee. He was sitting in his tentlike pajamas at a table when the phone rang.

"It's Nile."

Jessup forgot the food and concentrated on his man. "How did it go? Did you get the bastards?"

Barrabas brought him up to date on the most recent sinking.

"Something stinks there. Sounds like they had both trawlers wired to blow."

"That's my guess," Barrabas said. "We want to go after them, Walker."

"I can't see Washington going for it."

"Then we'll go ourselves."

"Let's think about it, Nile. What the hell's so damned important? So they invaded our waters. They destroyed some oil derricks. Not enough to risk your life for," the big man said. "And you wouldn't get backing. Have to find a boat or a plane and go in and out yourself. It's just not worth it.''

"Will you ask?"

"I'll ask," Jessup promised.

"So that's it? We let the bastards get away with it?''

"Not exactly. We've got hundreds of satellite shots of the trawlers and the action," Jessup said. "We got the testimony of the Yupiks. The CIA have a former Greenpeace Frenchman at Langley who will swear the French paid off a man called Beaudreau and he sold out to the Russians.'' He stopped to look longingly at the food. "Now, if we had their leaders, or someone pulling the strings . . . just maybe.''

The bells were going off in Barrabas's head. "What about the guys who blew the trawlers? They're still in the crashed chopper.''

"Can you get to it?''

"Piece of cake for Nanos and Hayes. If the Russkies don't decide to start World War III, that is.''

"Let's go with that. Maybe the bastards in the chopper can be identified. Better than a trip to their base on the peninsula only to learn that the man who engineered the job is under a hundred feet or so of water off our coast.''

"Will you get the red tape out of the way? We're all sitting here chewing our nails. Let's get with it, okay?''

"I'll call the senator right away. Should be about one in the morning in Washington. The bastard never sleeps, anyway.''

THE SENATOR and the DCI sat at a wooden table in the Capitol Hill office, steaming cups of coffee in front of them.

"That's the whole story," the senator concluded. "Instead of a single raid to discredit Greenpeace, they pulled four. I'm convinced someone in the KGB wanted some real damage to our Alaska oil installations."

"They didn't do badly, if you ask me," the Director of Central Intelligence said.

"And we can never *prove* it," the senator said, shifting in his chair and reaching for the coffee cup. "Sure, we have satellite pictures. But they made sure the physical evidence was destroyed. It's all under dark, cold water. My crew want to take it to them. To capture the commander of the raids on Russian soil." His eyes blazed. "I'm inclined to agree with them."

"Do we have any alternatives?" the DCI asked.

"One. The man who runs the team for me thinks he can recover the bodies of the men who went down in the helicopter."

"What the hell does that do for us?" the DCI, ever an opponent of the senator, asked.

"It's obvious the men in the helicopter used a remote-control device to destroy the trawlers and all physical evidence. That job wouldn't be entrusted to subordinates. If we get the bodies, they may be identified from the Agency's files of foreign agents.

"We bring them ashore. They've been in frigid waters for only a matter of hours. Assuming they were not badly mangled by the explosion that crippled their craft, they may be on file in the Agency's computer.''

"True." The DCI nodded. "We get prints from drinking glasses at social functions. Many of the top KGB people have been minor officials in Washington in the past. We've got their prints and pictures on file.''

"If you will keep a team on the alert at Langley, my people can send intelligence direct from the Bell 222's sophisticated computer systems. Takes only seconds,'' the senator said.

"Will Ivan stand by while we bring up the bodies of the men?''

The senator squirmed in his wheelchair. "No guarantees," he said. "They could harass our people with jets, gunships or even surface craft," he said, trying to keep his voice level.

"Sounds too risky," the head of Central Intelligence said.

"But if we pull it off, and the man at the controls turns out to be someone we can identify,'' the senator went on with enthusiasm, "his identity and our satellite pictures will condemn them in the international press.''

"Squadrons of fighters? Ships of the line? Gunships?'' the DCI muttered. "It would be like another Cuban blockade.''

"With one difference. The wreck is less than a mile offshore. Our waters. If they go after us, it will be in our home territory," the senator continued. "I think the first secretary tried a magnificent bluff, and it's worked up to now. I think he'll try one more...muster up all the hardware, but I don't think it'll be more than a bluff. He'd be stupid to start something, and we all know he's not stupid."

"I think we can work something out," the DCI said finally.

"Then do it. I'll get the Secretary of Defense behind us," the senator concluded, punching the button on the arm of his wheelchair and reaching for the telephone.

THE PHONE RANG in the community hut at about four in the morning. Barrabas grunted, roused himself from a half sleep and reached for it.

"Yeah?" he grunted.

"Walker. They been talking through the night, and they don't want a full-scale attack by your troops. They went for the salvage job."

"Okay. We'll get at it at first light. Get the people at the base to ship up two sets of scuba gear and extra tanks," the white-haired man said. "And get on to the Coast Guard. We'll need a boat after all. Something we can anchor over the wreckage and use as a diving platform. Nanos and Hayes will go down. Bishop and Beck will give us air cover, and the rest of us will be on the ship."

"Some people in Washington think the Soviets will pull a big bluff and harass you some."

"We'll hold our fire if they hold theirs."

"Don't let it get out of hand, Nile," the big man warned.

"We've never played poker together, Walker, or you'd know better. We'll keep it cool."

"The sea and sky could be full of bogeys," Walker said, his tone dead serious.

"And what will our people be doing...the military?" Barrabas asked.

"The same damned thing as the Russkies. Could get crowded as hell up there. A lot of people have been roused from their beds tonight: the Secretary of Defense; the chairman of the Joint Chiefs; the Secretary of State. The Hill's been buzzing—all closed doors, of course," the fat Texan went on. "They know the score, and they're not going to be bluffed down."

"Sounds like quite a show. And we'll have a front-row seat," Barrabas said.

"Take care, Nile."

"Will do."

"Wait. One last thing," the fat man said. "When you bring them up, Langley will be standing by to take info from Nate over the chopper's systems. Fingerprints, facial features...that sort of thing."

"Nate's done it before. He can handle it."

"Luck, Nile. Don't fall overboard."

"About as much chance of that as of you going on a diet," Barrabas chuckled as he hung up.

They were all going to enjoy having one last crack at it. He thought about the warnings of the fat man. It might be quite a show. If they started a shooting war up there, it would spread all over the globe.

## 15

At about six in the morning the SOBs began to stir in their lodge next to Charlie's cabin. It wasn't dawn. Full daylight would not stream through the windows for hours.

Breakfast was set up at Charlie's. He wasn't going to the last battle, so he rose early to stand over the old wood stove, cooking platters of Canadian bacon and fried eggs.

Barrabas was content. The wreck of the helicopter wasn't going anywhere, dawn was still a couple of hours away, and he wanted his warriors to start with full bellies.

"What time is the shipment arriving?" Bishop asked, reaching for a piece of the crusty local bread.

"Jessup told them nine. We'll have daylight from nine to about four today," the colonel answered. "How does that sound, Claude? Enough time to bring them up?"

"Tell you better after a test dive, Colonel," Hayes said.

"Don't know how deep the dive will be," Nanos joined in, holding a forkful of bacon close to his mouth.

"Let's hope seven hours will be enough. It's going to be a bad time," Barrabas said, a frown creasing his tanned face.

They ate in silence for a few minutes.

"You think they'll have a look?" Hatton asked, breaking the silence.

"Wouldn't you?" Barrabas asked. "The Russians are not fools. They'll be monitoring by satellite just as we have. When they see us over the crash site, they'll know what's going down."

Another silence followed as they ate and thought about the action to come. It wasn't their kind of action, and they didn't know what to expect.

"What's the worst that can happen?" Beck finally asked. He never ate breakfast, but sat over his third cup of coffee, waiting for the others.

"The worst?" Barrabas thought, screwing up his face as he swallowed some egg. "Both sides saturate the area with the biggest and best hardware they've got, and someone makes a mistake."

"Like pressing the button?" Billy asked.

"You've got it. Like pressing the button. Don't think it can't happen," Barrabas warned.

They sat around the huge wooden table, each with his own thoughts. Charlie had begun to clear away the dirty plates. He put a fresh pot of coffee on the table. The first streaks of light crept through the windows, a weak challenge for the naked bulbs that lit the scene.

"Colonel, I could help..." their host started.

"No, Charlie. We appreciate your offer. But this is not for you," Barrabas responded.

Charlie continued to clear the table as they rose, one after the other, and pulled on their outer clothing. He didn't offer any further comment.

As they were about to leave, the Eskimo's radio came alive. He handed it to Barrabas.

"It's me, Nile." It was Jessup's voice. "I've got a ride with the Army people, and I'll see you at the site."

"What the hell for?" Barrabas asked, totally surprised.

"I'm tired of this damned hotel room. I'm going to be in on it."

"Forget it. Nothing you can do."

"I'm coming, anyway. I'm so close, why not?"

"I'll tell you why, dammit. First, we don't need a passenger on this. More important, we want someone we can trust at the other end of the line. Jesus! We need you to clear with the senator."

"Clear what, for chrissakes?"

"Walker, you're not thinking. Anything can happen when we make the dive. We have to check for official sanction on this one. Suppose they fire on us? Could be accidental or deliberate. What the hell do we do? Could be a thousand things." Barrabas was insistent.

"Shit! You're probably right. But this place is like a morgue."

"We'll probably heat it up for you. Stay close to the radio. Make sure the senator and anyone he has to get to are standing by. This one is about as political as it gets.''

''Are your people okay?'' Jessup asked.

''They feel strange. I can feel it. They're fighters like me. This is a new one for us.''

''Well. I'll be here. Call me whether you need help or not, okay?''

''Will do.'' Barrabas switched off and turned to the others who had been listening. ''Let's get with it,'' he said.

The 222 sat outside the hut about a hundred feet away on a flat outcrop of rock. The crash site was only about a half hour away by chopper.

DAWN WAS BREAKING, and the scene was bathed in its early glow. An official Army chopper sat close to shore, and a Coast Guard cutter at anchor rode the mild chop about a hundred feet out.

Bishop brought the Bell 222 down next to the chopper. While he was settling the skids, the Coast Guard launched two dinghies sending the crew ashore.

The Army crew, a captain and one sergeant, stood next to the chopper. They had unloaded three crates and were ready to take off.

The Coast Guard skeleton crew beached the dinghies, trotted to the Army chopper and climbed aboard. The captain signaled the sergeant, and, their faces showing their disapproval, they boarded the old Bell chopper and took off.

To hell with them. The SOBs had enough to think about without worrying about their feelings. ''So much for interservice cooperation," O'Toole said with disgust.

"Don't be naive, Liam," Barrabas said, smiling. "The Army people are ordered by their commanding general to make a delivery. A general, incidentally, who hates our guts. As for the Coast Guard," he went on, "eight strangers take over their vessel, one they've probably sweated over with mop and paintbrush. They probably think we're getting paid a bundle for this, and they're right."

While they were talking, Billy had ripped the top off all three crates. One was filled with scuba gear: wet suits, streamlined double tanks, intercom sets, nets, lines, goggles, mouthpieces. Another was intended to rearm the Bell 222. Someone had assumed it would need a whole complement of missiles and ammo. The third contained enough arms to equip a small army, from SMGs to small batteries of ground-to-air missiles.

"Correct me if I read you wrong, Colonel. Didn't you say last night we were to go in as quickly as possible, recover the bodies and get the hell out without firing a shot?" O'Toole asked.

"Seems to me your worst scenario isn't the same as those of the people supplying us," Hatton offered.

"Forget it," Barrabas said. "Would you like to stand around empty-handed while the enemy tries to harass you?"

"Is that what's going to happen?" Bishop asked.

"That's the way I see it," Barrabas said.

"But these are American waters," Beck protested.

"Makes it interesting, right?" Barrabas grinned. "Let's move it."

BISHOP AND BECK HAD BROUGHT the 222's armament to full strength, warmed her up and circled over the dive site, keeping no more than a mile between them and the cutter.

Hayes and Nanos, the diving experts, examined the scuba gear, selected what they needed and took it out to the cutter in one of the dinghies. They returned to pick up the other mercs, who had armed themselves heavily. The crates, still half-full, were abandoned on the rocky shore.

Nanos and Hayes took the rest of the SOBs aboard. They were pleased with the cutter. She was the USCGC *Petrel* (WSES-4). Originally designed for running down drug smugglers in Florida, she had found her way to northern waters. Anchored fore and aft, she had a sixty-foot steel hull at the waterline. The whole ship, including the twin diesels that could push her at thirty-five knots, was spotless.

The two men of the sea had dumped the scuba gear on the aft deck where the thwarts were only five feet from the rolling chop. While they pulled on the wet suits, Hayes explained to Barrabas what they intended.

"We think the crash site is between one and two hundred yards farther out. We're going to make a trial dive, and if we find the wreck, we'll loose a marker," he said as he pulled the black rubber cap over his short curly hair.

"Will we have to move the ship?" Barrabas asked.

"We'll come aboard for fresh tanks. Alex and I will move her and anchor over the wreck."

Nanos was ready. He blew through his lines to clear them. After coating the inside of his mask with his own saliva and rinsing it out, he sat on the gunwale, waiting for Hayes.

When they were both ready, Nanos fell backward into the black water, then they were both out of sight, their communication lines trailing after them.

IN THE WOODS OF MARYLAND, a tall man sat alone in an office paneled with white oak. He loved the room and spent as much time there as possible. On the desk in front of him were two telephones—one white and one red. Outside the door, another man sat patiently with a briefcase chained to his wrist. He was never more than a few feet away from The Man.

It was almost noon Maryland time. The action would just be getting underway in Alaska. Nevertheless, the craggy-faced gaunt giant was restless. He didn't want any of his staff near him. A stack of official documents tempted him to read, but the words blurred together as he failed to concentrate.

The burden of office had been evident from day one, but it hadn't been like the present. He imagined Jack Kennedy faced with the Bay of Pigs incident, or worse, the gut-wrenching decision to blockade Cuba during the missile crisis.

It was a lonesome job. Despite the democratic process, the final decision was his, and the load was almost overwhelming. He has seen his predecessors age twenty years during one term. He had looked in the mirror and noted the signs of the process in himself.

He felt just like he had before assuming office. But he didn't look the same. No matter how he foiled his inner self, he couldn't fool the shell that surrounded him. As had his predecessors, he had aged rapidly. Again he acknowledged to himself that the burden was almost too much.

His next thoughts were about the first secretary, his counterpart in the Soviet Union. He had met the Soviet leader, and they had talked through interpreters for hours. But there had been no real understanding between the leaders.

How could there be? The first secretary was dedicated to making his people, in the guise of ideology, the masters of the world. It was monstrous. The chief executive found it hard to accept that the Communist leaders believed in their own philosophy when it was obvious the system didn't even work in their own country. The tall American felt that it was ludicrous to constantly work toward world peace, the feeding and nurturing of the world's hungry, and at the same time fight an enemy who had such cold determination.

What made the foremost man of the USSR think the way he did? What was he thinking right now? He had pulled an audacious bluff and crippled some of America's Alaskan oil facilities. In the process, world opinion had come to blame the French. Many world leaders were gullible—ready to believe anything. Even if some—the most intelligent—recognized his devious hand in it, they couldn't prove it. So the ploy had been effective.

But maybe the Russians hadn't won. If it could be proved, beyond all doubt, that their leader had engineered the attacks on the Alaska facilities, the adverse international publicity would irreparably harm the credibility of the USSR. Proving them aggressors who had attacked the American mainland would provide leverage in future summits and turn the tide in many countries that were on the verge of converting to Communism.

The possibilities were endless.

Satellite photos of the fake Greenpeace ships weren't conclusive enough, nor was a witness who could tell the story about Beaudreau. Along with the story of the Yupiks who had been trained within Russia for the raids, the evidence so far was strong.

But it wasn't enough.

One truly damning piece of evidence was vital to show that the whole operation was controlled by the Russians.

The tall man pondered what he would do if a shooting war started over the search he had ordered. He really didn't know. As he stood to stir the ashes in the fireplace and throw on another log, he accepted that he had no clue what he would do.

He wondered by what process George Washington had made his most momentous decisions. How had

Lincoln coped with the tremendous burden of an internal struggle? What had been Jack Kennedy's method of handling the pressure?

Was he about to find out?

## 16

The dark green water was cut by the two high-powered lamps Nanos and Hayes had strapped to their heads. They circled the *Petrel*, keeping about twenty feet from her hull. At thirty feet they did a second sweep without seeing anything. After deciding the inshore leg of the search was the wrong direction, they concentrated on deeper water.

The shore sheared off more sharply than they had expected. They were only forty yards beyond the ship when they were searching the bottom at one hundred feet.

The water was alive with fish. Along the stony bottom the two divers found the sea rich with crustaceans, large crabs and a kind of Arctic lobster with miniature claws. But no wreckage.

Time passed quickly. They watched their counters carefully and surfaced with only five minutes left in their tanks. They had covered only about seventy yards out.

On the surface, Billy Two and O'Toole, both restless, helped pull their friends aboard and lifted off the spent tanks.

"Anything at all?" Barrabas asked.

"Not yet," Nanos said, accepting a mug of steaming coffee from Lee Hatton.

"What the hell's been going on up here?" Hayes asked, looking around, surprised at the noise.

"Some company," Barrabas said matter-of-factly. "Started to gather as soon as you dived."

"Who are they?" Nanos asked, ignoring the steaming mug in his hand.

"The small carrier to port is ours." Barrabas had his glasses trained on her. "She's the USS *Belleau Wood*. Came in after the Russian fighters started to circle."

"I know her," Hayes broke in. "Eight hundred and twenty feet. She can take CH-53s or CH-46s for routine search and attack. She's also designed to take Harrier AV-8Bs."

"The fighters tracing figure eights over us are the best in the world," Barrabas went on. "We should feel honored. F-16s out of Eielson—refueling pods, AIM-9Js and four missiles."

He traversed to the starboard side. "The Russians sent a squadron of Foxbats. They are equivalent to about MiG-40s—deadly—carry eight missiles and long-range pods. Could get real heated up in the next couple hours."

THOUSANDS OF MILES TO THE WEST, in the heart of Moscow, a lone man sat in a luxurious office, mulling over the news he'd just received. The Americans had made their move. They were diving to recover Petrov's helicopter.

Petrov had been a damned fool to be shot down! But it was too late for recriminations. Mesmerof, too, was a fool—an old and used-up one. He couldn't be trusted to carry through with the rest of the plan. So, what the hell was the first secretary to do?

The red telephone on his desk was a stark reminder of the constant war he waged. The phone often proved to be a motivator. He wouldn't touch it, but would look at it when he was alone, and it would strengthen his resolve.

At the salvage site, off the Alaska Arctic shelf, where his attack had been intended to destroy the American experimental station, the enemy had brought in a small carrier and a squadron of F-16s. His local commander had countered with a squadron of Foxbats with orders to observe only. That was a move to be applauded, but it was not enough.

He pressed the button on his intercom. An aide answered immediately.

"Yes, First Secretary."

"Get Marshal Dubinsky in here at once. If he's not in Moscow, get his second-in-command—Dobrovski. And bring me coffee with some cognac."

The first secretary considered the situation along the Arctic Shelf. His people were in American waters. A dangerous scenario. The red phone could ring at any moment, and he'd have to talk to the American President again. He hated the man. The cold blue eyes that he'd stared at over conference tables haunted him.

While he tried to wipe out the memory of those penetrating eyes, his aide came in with fresh coffee and a bottle of cognac. The man was young to be a colonel. But then, he was brilliant. He would be with the first secretary for a long time—if they muddled through. The young man poured a black coffee and topped it with a couple of ounces of cognac, just the way the older man liked it. Leaving the tray on the desk, the aide headed for the door without a word.

One of the man's best qualities, the first secretary thought. When asked, the young man had intelligent answers. But when he wasn't consulted, he kept his mouth shut—a lesson that the first secretary wished half his colleagues in the Presidium had learned years ago.

He was halfway through the cup of brew when the door opened and Marshal Dubinsky was shown in.

"Sit, Anatole, old friend. I'm having a coffee and cognac. Pour yourself one."

"Thank you, First Secretary. Very kind."

It was a mark of the Soviet leader's power that the oldest of his friends, the ones alongside whom he had climbed to power, always addressed him by his formal title. He called them by their first names when so inclined but never allowed the same intimacy to be returned.

"You know about the action on the Alaska Arctic Shelf." It was a statement, not a question.

"Yes. I think my man's strategy was good," the marshal said.

"I agree. I want you to go further—I want a real show of force up there. Make it look good."

"It's a long way from our main bases, and it will take time."

*"We don't have any time."* The words had been expelled with tight-lipped force.

"I'll do the best I can." The marshal paled under the wrath of his former friend.

The first secretary cooled his temper. "I know you will, Anatole. We must put on a strong show."

"But without firing," the marshal reminded.

The man behind the ornate desk thought for a moment. "What, in your opinion, would be the consequence if we shot down the helicopter over the wreck, or sent a missile into the salvage ship?" he asked.

The marshal's face was completely drained of blood. "All-out war? Maybe conventional, maybe nuclear. I don't trust that bastard in the White House."

"Nor do I," the first secretary agreed. "Still..."

They talked for half an hour, sometimes resorting to the phone, and gradually learned that a fair-sized armada could be mustered in the waters not far from the salvage vessel.

"I must get back to my office, First Secretary. I'd like to control this from the War Room."

Located next to the marshal's office, the War Room was a large conference hall—a cocoon the top military people used as a hideaway. The first secretary merely nodded his agreement and drained the last of his second cup of brew.

When the marshal had gone, the Soviet leader brooded for a long time about the plan he had started.

It could still work, and probably would. The Americans had no real proof that the world would accept as being conclusive. Now if they had Petrov, that would be another matter. But they wouldn't get him. Not a chance.

BARRABAS STOOD at the aft deck. His men had gone down for their third dive. He waited. It was past noon, and they had about three and a half hours of daylight left.

The buildup of ships and planes had continued unabated since the first dive. Barrabas could hardly believe it. On the American side, two FSSs—Fast Sealift Ships—had appeared and anchored beside the carrier. Two *Ticonderoga*-class missile cruisers had appeared from the south and patrolled back and forth one thousand yards from his position. If his hunt extended that far, he'd have to radio them to stand off.

On the Russian side, two *Kiev*-class missile cruisers had taken up position farther out to sea a hundred yards beyond and matched the *Ticonderoga*s in their constant vigil. A trio of *Krivak III* class frigates cruised dangerously close to the FSSs and the *Belleau Wood*. Except for the billions of dollars' worth of fighters overhead, the whole scene reminded Barrabas of his childhood at school when small gangs challenged each other to rumbles, using sticks and stones. The challenges were mostly show. The rumbles seldom happened, but when they did, they were damned bloody.

He had just completed the thought when a brace of Foxbats buzzed Bishop and Beck, who were circling overhead. They had barely started their pass when a squadron of F/A-18s gave chase. An air battle followed, complete with all the maneuvers of crack pilots, but without the deadly firepower that usually goes with it.

THE TALL MAN PACED for a few minutes, then he sat down and reached for the red phone. Of all his official duties, it was the most dreaded.

"First Secretary," he asked. He heard the translation in the background.

"Mr. President," the translator responded.

"You have military aircraft—aircraft with no clearance—flying over American soil."

"A mistake. It has been explained to me. Maybe you care to state why your military aircraft followed them into Soviet air space."

"Repelling invaders. Nothing more." The tall man's voice was cold and would always be cold when dealing with what the Russian leader stood for.

"Your carrier and missile-carrying ships are close to our shores. Surely that is a provocation."

"Let's talk straight," the President said. "The United States of America didn't start the provocation, and didn't ask to lose Alaska oil. But the USSR couldn't pass up the aggression. It will only take one more shot for the United States to respond with force.

"I speak from a position of strength, with the backing of my people. We won't hesitate to return fire.

We intend to salvage your downed aircraft from our waters and give the men a decent burial."

"A lie, Mr. President. Your intention is to use him to discredit us. I will announce your devious plot to the international press before the wreck is raised."

The use of "him" instead of "them" alerted the President, but he didn't pause to analyse it. "When we raise the wreck, we will have enough to thoroughly justify our action to the press," he said. "The next time we meet across a table, the balance of power will reflect this instance of bad judgment."

The President hung up the receiver and thought about the mess he was in. He had challenged the Russian leader. Did he, as the leader of America, have the guts to carry through? He thought so. But God forbid it should come to that.

Then he thought about the first secretary's use of the pronoun "him." It seemed to confirm that definite proof to implicate the Kremlin—probably the body of a high-ranking KGB man—would be recovered from the helicopter. That slip of the tongue had been the final clue.

The President intended to keep the secret knowledge to himself. Others in Washington wouldn't interpret it as he had. His shoulders felt the lessening of the load. He knew he was getting closer. Hot Damn!

HIS TWO MEN had ranged so far afield that Barrabas had lost sight of the air bubbles. The buildup continued. Missiles bristled from every direction. If a shooting war started now, it would be carnage. No one would escape.

As if on a signal, the false dogfights stopped. While he was considering that, an orange marker bobbed to the surface, not far from the patrolling American cruisers.

He waited for Hayes and Nanos to return and relocate the ship closer to the marker. Then he called Jessup from the radio room and told the Texan to have the American cruisers stand off. Hayes and Nanos had found the wreck.

WHILE BARRABAS TALKED TO JESSUP, a KGB agent was talking to a rear admiral on one of the *Kiev*-class cruisers.

"They have found the wreckage. We spotted a marker buoy ten minutes ago. What do you want us to do?"

"Nothing. Not yet. Keep your distance, and I will call Mesmerof."

The agent called the private number and was put through immediately.

"They've found the wreck. What do we do?"

"We try what we discussed."

"But..."

"We try it. It either works or it doesn't."

**17**

Hayes and Nanos were peeling off their wet suits on the fantail. Everyone else on board, except Barrabas, scanned the water around them for signs of the enemy. With the Soviet ships so close, they looked for signs of enemy frogmen or miniature subs in the area.

"We've got almost three hours of daylight left," Barrabas said. "How long to retrieve the bodies?"

"No sweat, Colonel," Hayes answered. "Move the ship. Dive once more. Less than two hours."

"Okay. Take your time. I'll tell the others."

He went forward to check with O'Toole. "How's it going?" he asked the big Irish-American.

"I think it's a waste of time, Colonel. No way they're going to hit us here. If they send out frogmen, it's going to be at the dive site."

"Tell Lee and Billy to give it a rest. One of the three of you can keep watch alone. We're going to move the ship now, anyway."

While they talked, Nanos moved to the wheelhouse and started the two powerful diesels. He revved to smooth them out, and when they were at low revs again, he backed a few feet.

Hayes, at the stern, had one foot on the electric anchor winch. He fed the chain into an aft locker as it snaked from the water.

The stern swung with the current toward shore as the big black man secured the aft anchor and walked to the bow. Nanos rode her up on the forward anchor while Hayes winched it in.

Slowly Nanos brought her about, and with just enough way to maneuver. Within minutes, they came up to the bobbing marker. They had moved almost five hundred yards and were close to the *Ticonderoga* cruisers.

Hayes dropped the aft anchor and fed out chain. Nanos slowed her until she had almost lost way while Hayes dropped the forward anchor. With the big diesels in reverse, Nanos let her slide back on the forward chain while Hayes took up slack on the aft anchor. The ship rode at a right angle to the shore, taking the light inshore chop on her bows.

WHILE THE TWO SOB DIVERS prepared to go down again, a separate show was taking place farther out to sea. The *Ticonderoga*-class cruisers moved to give the SOB ship room to maneuver, approaching the *Kiev*-class cruisers.

The Russians held their positions, patrolling back and forth parallel to the coast. The ships of two navies, ships worth billions of dollars, played a game of chicken, passing each other with no more than twenty feet of white water between them. They used their air horns constantly, shouting back and forth. The hoot-

hoot of the horns and the voices that floated over Arctic waters added to the constant scream of jets overhead. On the deck of the *Petrel*, communication was almost impossible.

Nanos and Hayes eased back into black water, the light from their lamps producing narrow beams as they churned through ice-cold liquid on the way down. It was no place for someone with claustrophobia. Almost any merc would prefer the cold sweat of a firefight to gliding through the frigid waters with nothing but the pencil beam of light to follow.

Firefights were sometimes a mystery. A man seldom knew the odds he faced or the firepower the enemy controlled. But he could see the terrain. He saw the enemy.

The two mercs didn't know what to expect. And they couldn't see worth a damn.

BARRABAS HAD WATCHED his men submerge and was about to turn to the others when he noticed that the marker buoy bobbed like a fisherman's float and then went under. He waited for it to bob to the surface, but it didn't appear.

"Alex!" he shouted over the intercom. "The float's disappeared. Something took it. It hasn't shown again."

"Got you, Colonel."

Now what the hell, the big Greek thought. A fish could have taken the line or even the marker, but that was very unusual. It had to be something else...

something he couldn't see and wouldn't see until he got down to the wreck.

And by then it might be too late. Too late for him to see. Too late to take evasive action.

Despite the power in Nanos's legs, developed from hours of muscle work, Hayes scissored past him, following the rope faster than the force that pulled it.

Hayes carried a crowbar in his belt. Following the rope to the bottom, he found a chain secured to the wrecked tail section of the Russian chopper. She was being slowly winched out to sea.

Through the muck swirling from the disturbed bottom, he could vaguely see the shape of the two divers who had connected the chain to the chopper. He cut his light so he wouldn't be seen if they looked back to guide the leading edge of the chopper.

He called through the intercom. "Alex! You read me?"

"Yeah. I'm trying to keep up. You're going too damned fast."

"I'm near the wreck. The Russians are trying to winch her away, Alex," Hayes said urgently through the intercom. "Catch up if you can. I'm going to pry a door open and pull out the bodies." His voice was ragged from heavy breathing, and the transmission was poor. "We can pick them out of the muck later."

BARRABAS HEARD EVERY WORD. He was on the horn to Jessup. "Get me patched in to the commander of the missile cruiser force. It's urgent."

"Why. What the hell's going down?" The fat man fidgeted in his hotel room in Fairbanks. He'd have given anything to be in the middle of the action.

"The chopper is being winched away," Barrabas yelled impatiently. "Something down there's taking the damned evidence. One of the *Kiev* cruisers must have launched a landing craft. They couldn't be doing it from the mother ship."

"So what do you want our people to do? Blow it out of the water?"

"Blow the damned thing! Launch one of their landing craft! Anything!"

"No way!" the fat man said. "Get Bishop to have a look. He can buzz them or something. No one's going to tell the *Ticonderoga* captains to take action."

"You tell them to take action, or I'll have Bishop blow whatever it is out of the water. They're taking the wreck right from under our noses, for chrissakes."

"Cool it, Nile. You're not going to shoot. Is that clear? No one is going to shoot."

"Shit!" Barrabas snatched at the radio and switched over to Bishop's frequency.

"Come in, Geoff. Make it fast!"

"Yeah, Colonel."

"What the hell's going on? Is there a smaller boat out there with the cruisers?"

"One of the *Kiev* cruisers launched a landing craft. I was just trying to get you."

"Well, stop the bastard. He's winching in the wreck. I don't know what's happened to our guys down below."

"You want me to blow him out of the water? Could start a shooting war."

"No. Buzz the bastard. Get him to release the winch. Get as close as you can."

HAYES PULLED HIMSELF FORWARD in the swirl of muck from the bottom. He could hear the propellers of the missile cruisers overhead. He pulled the crowbar from his belt and with his free arm attempted to wedge open the bent Plexiglas door. It was like trying to break through steel.

Replacing the crowbar in his belt, he pulled himself forward against the constant drag. Then he twisted the handle.

Nothing. The wrecked chopper moved forward with the pull of the winch.

Hayes held on with one hand, the debris of the ocean floor sliding past in a steady, slimy stream. He reached for the crowbar again.

He couldn't see anything and didn't know how long he'd been down there. It seemed like forever. He was short on air, and it was a long way back.

The powerful black man slipped the crowbar into the crack of the door and heaved. It opened a little. He heaved again, and it widened a few inches.

The drift didn't help. It pulled at the door, trying to close it. With a superhuman effort, Hayes pulled the door farther open and swam inside.

He took a chance and switched on his light for a few seconds. One body was wedged behind the controls, and the other was on the floor next to the far door. Scores of sea creatures scurried past him, brushing his wet suit and hitting his head, slanting the ray of his light in their frantic escape through the open door.

ALEX NANOS PUMPED his powerful thighs and cursed. The rubber fins on his feet pushed him as fast as he could go, but he couldn't catch up to Hayes. Visibility was all but nonexistent because of the churned-up debris. He wasn't sure where the chopper was but kept on going in the direction in which Claude had disappeared a few minutes earlier.

His light was useless in the swirling muck from the sea floor. He turned it off and was immediately enveloped in the total black of the deep.

He had no idea how long he'd been swimming. His leg muscles felt a definite strain. He didn't know how much air he had left, and he didn't know where the hell he was or how far it was back to the ship.

He turned on the light again.

Swimming at full speed, he collided with something that came at him from the darkness. It hit him solidly and wrapped its tentacles around him. His legs were trapped. He struggled, using the muscles he'd developed to perfection, but he couldn't fight the foreign body holding him. Pushed against him by the current, it held him fast.

A cold chill moved up his spine, and he tried to struggle. He began to float clear of the swirl of muck until he could see dim glow from the sky. He looked around. At first he couldn't see anything, and he was still held prisoner by the tentacles around him.

Then his light, swiveling back and forth as he moved his head, shone on a ghoulish object. A mass of pulpy flesh floated past his face mask. A head appeared. A face. A horror mask, little more than strings of flesh and white bone.

CLAUDE MANAGED TO FREE the pilot and throw him from the towed wreck. It was a hell of a job. The feet had been jammed beneath the controls, and Hayes had broken both the dead man's shinbones in the process.

Now the pilot was out. The body drifted from the wreck, pushed by the current toward Nanos.

Hayes was left with the passenger. He tugged the corpse free of the floor and managed to get it on the seat. The noise of the propellers was louder overhead, and he hurriedly pulled on one arm and slipped from the wreck. The body floated after him. As his hand slid down the uniformed sleeve, Hayes tried to get a firmer grip. The arm felt more like bone than solid flesh as he pulled the bloated body free of its crushed metal coffin.

At last no foreign force was pulling him in the opposite direction. He put both hands under the armpits of his charge and finned slowly upward, away from the silt below.

"Alex. Can you read me?" Hayes asked.

"Barely. Where the hell are you?"

"I got one of the bodies from the wreck. I'm below the missile cruisers, but damned if I know which way to head out."

"I got the other body. I'm halfway between the cruisers and our ship. Got just enough air in my tanks to get me back."

"Great. I'm farther out. Probably don't have enough air."

Barrabas broke in. "Can you see the sky, Claude?"

"Sure. I can see daylight enough. Probably about fifty feet down. But I'm under the path of the cruisers."

"We're going to fire a couple of flares. If you see them, they should give you a direct path to us."

"I'm watching," Claude said.

Barrabas ordered O'Toole to fire flares directly at the missile cruisers, but to have them fall short by about fifty feet. He ran for the fantail and began to put on a wet suit.

Lee Hatton followed him.

"Can I help, Colonel?" she asked.

"Find out if Claude sees the flares while I'm suiting up," the white-haired man said as he pulled the wet suit past his hips. "If he sees them, tell him to put on his own light and watch for mine. We'll come up on the buddy system."

Ten minutes later, fifty feet down, Barrabas saw Nanos's light, and then he saw the big Greek. He was towing a body in a direction that would put him close enough to the ship. Barrabas didn't stop.

It seemed like forever but had been only twenty minutes. That was all right for him. But Hayes had been down more than half an hour, and he had to be out of air.

He churned faster, heading for the cruisers and staying as close to the bottom as he could. His light cut a path from left to right through the silty water as he swiveled his head.

He'd lost sight of Hayes's communication line, and he could see no other divers. The shapes of missile cruisers loomed overhead.

Then it flashed at him. Directly ahead, a light shone from the clouds of muck. He headed straight toward it.

Claude was on the bottom, still holding on to the dead man.

Barrabas looked through the black man's visor. His friend smiled slackly. He was about as far gone as he could be without losing it. The colonel slipped out his mouthpiece and fitted it over Hayes's mouth.

Slowly the big man's eyes cleared. He looked more like the vital merc who had fought at his side so many times. Hayes signaled for Barrabas to take his turn at the air by passing the mouthpiece back.

LEE HATTON STOOD on the fantail and watched for her people to come back. She saw nothing. She climbed to the control room and called Bishop.

"Geoff. Come in." Her voice penetrated the static from the poor transmission caused by scores of jet engines still screaming overhead. "It's Lee."

"I read you. What's up?"

"Forget the surface craft. We got more troubles," she said. "It's Claude. I think Alex is going to make it back, but Claude must be almost out of air, and he's out by the cruisers. The colonel has gone after him."

"I'll make a slow circuit."

She watched as he circled the waters between her and the cruisers as slowly as he could.

"Best I can do is one set of bubbles approaching you," the Canadian airman reported. "About twenty yards out."

"Thanks. Keep an eye out for the others, okay?"

"Got you."

She ran to the fantail and searched the water for the first set of bubbles. Nanos broke the surface about ten feet out and stroked the rest of the way. With the last of his strength, he pushed one of the dead man's arms at Lee and held on to the gunwale.

Billy Two appeared at Lee's side, and they hauled the dead man over the rear thwarts. Then Billy grabbed his friend and hoisted him aboard with one hand.

IT WAS SLOW, but it was working. Barrabas had taken over the weight of the dead man from the exhausted Hayes, and they shared the air on their slow ascent. The sky overhead had darkened, and they couldn't see as well. Barrabas knew they were on the right heading. It was just a matter of time.

He could see the ship's form overhead. It was maybe one hundred feet away. His arms felt like lead.

Fifty more feet. Twenty. Then he felt his burden taken from him and strong hands under his shoulders hauling him aboard. He flopped onto the steel plating of the deck like a beached fish and stayed motionless for a few minutes. No hurry now. It was still daylight, and they had their prize.

## 18

Minutes went by with only the sounds of the sea and harsh breathing. Barrabas, Nanos and Hayes slowly gathered strength and sat up. They looked into the faces of Lee, Billy Two and Liam, expecting them to be smiling, happy to see them. The heroes of the deep. They looked as if they had lost the battle instead of winning it.

"What the hell's the matter with you? We got what we were looking for," Barrabas said.

In answer, O'Toole flipped one of the bodies over with his foot. The face was a mass of scarred flesh and white bone. Hatton picked up an arm and showed the colonel an almost empty sleeve. All he could see was white bone.

"Crabs," Lee said. "Crabs, lobsters. Crustaceans will do this every time."

They had never thought of flesh-eating crabs. They had expected that the bodies might have been mutilated beyond recognition by the missile, but not this. They would still call in Beck and get him to transmit what he could to Washington, but it didn't look good.

Barrabas stripped off his wet suit and headed for the radio in the control room when he was distracted by a change in the constant noise of jets overhead.

One of the Foxbats had broken formation and was making a missile run straight at them.

The SOBs all caught the move at the same time and ran to pick up discarded weapons. Before they had the weapons in hand, they realized it was too late. They were sitting ducks.

The Russians had planned a two-pronged attack. They were willing to chance a shooting war to destroy the evidence, not knowing the crabs had done their work for them.

Beck watched the Foxbat formation from the chopper. The Foxbat fired.

Beck hit the release button for a missile while the Bell 222 was in the exact attitude for maximum results. The sunburst trajectory took it directly to the nose of the Russian missile. The explosion rained debris over the Coast Guard cutter. Jagged pieces of shrapnel tore the roof of the control room apart.

Bishop moved the nose of the Bell 222 to follow the flight of the Foxbat as she dived past the SOBs' ship.

He fired. A rocket sped straight at the Foxbat, breathing fire down her tail as she skimmed across the water.

At the last second, the Foxbat pilot pulled up into a screaming climb.

Bishop's rocket hit the water behind the sleek fighter.

The SOBs watched the Foxbat rejoin its group and heard the screaming of F/A-18 jets as they made a pass at the Foxbat squadron. The cruisers were more belligerent than ever. They separated, forming battle positions with missile systems constantly trained on each other.

A group of five Harrier V/STOL fighters came screaming in from the carrier to hover above the *Petrel*, giving it protective cover. They were no more than fifty feet off the deck, forming a circle around the ship about one hundred yards in diameter. Communication below was impossible while the Harriers were in their vertical flight attitudes and hovering.

Barrabas stumbled to the ruined control room and reached for the radio. "Bishop," he said. "Come on in, Geoff."

"Loud and clear, Colonel."

"We'll see you on the beach," he said. "We'll send what we've got to Washington."

Next he called Jessup. "Walker!" he shouted over the noise of F/A-18s returning to their cruising altitudes. "A close one up here. One of their jets fired a missile at us. Beck destroyed the missile, and Bishop fired at the Foxbat."

"Damned fool!"

"Hold on, Walker. Geoff reacted the same as we all would. He didn't score a hit on the enemy craft," Barrabas said. "What I want you to do is to call off this whole buildup. You give a blood-and-guts general so much hardware near the enemy, and sooner or later he'll find an excuse for using it—in spades. Call it all off, Walker, whatever you have to do. Get all the bastards to take off and leave us alone.''

"What about the salvage?''

"Got them both out, but it doesn't look good. Sea creatures got to them first. I don't think you've got a hope of identifying them.''

"Damn! That was important. The whole mission is a waste if we don't.''

"Maybe not a dead loss. Beck's still going to send what he can.''

"Good. As a backup, I'll get the CIA to pick up the bodies. We'll have them flown back to Langley by special jet. Pick them up at Charlie's. You go back there and wait.''

"Why don't we get transport from Eielson to Washington?'' Barrabas asked. "You want us to go in if Langley comes up with nothing?''

"I have to wait for the word.''

"I HAD GIVEN WARNING, First Secretary,'' the tall man said into the mouthpiece of the red phone. "Now you have attacked one of our ships in Alaska waters.''

"An overeager pilot. He will be disciplined,'' the voice of the interpreter intoned without emotion.

The man in the log cabin hated the sound of the interpreter's voice. He felt as though he was talking to a recording. He couldn't even hear the first secretary speaking Russian in the background. The whole process was cold and impersonal, just like the Russians.

It was the part of his job he truly disliked. Dealing with Middle East problems, he could feel the emotion. Even at social events in Moscow and at the Russian embassy, when the Russians were at their most garrulous and friendly, he felt as though they had been wound up like robots and turned loose to perform.

"That lacks credibility," he said. "I've been kept current on your actions. First, there was the attempt to tow away the crashed helicopter. Then, a deliberate maneuver to get rid of the evidence by destroying the salvage ship."

"You stretch the fact. It is our helicopter."

"In our waters."

"I demand the return of the bodies of our heroic men immediately. We will send a landing craft ashore," the bland voice continued.

"I'll tell you what you do," the President said with deadly calmness. "Remove your equipment. Your men's remains will be examined in Washington. Then, maybe, they'll be shipped home.

"Let me tell you, First Secretary," the President went on. "I have never felt so strongly about any of your covert actions as I do about this." The face of the tall man flushed as he spoke. "You sent men to destroy property in the guise of Greenpeace volunteers. The world will know as soon as I can get the facts out.

"Our attitude at the bargaining table will be tougher in future. And—" his voice was implacable "—there must be an immediate withdrawal beyond your borders."

He slammed down the receiver. He was sweating profusely. Pulling out a large white handkerchief, he wiped his face. He had issued the final ultimatum.

He put the handkerchief away and reached for the buzzer beside his desk. A male secretary appeared and waited for instructions.

"Tell the Secretary of Defense to have our people stand down in Alaska when the Russians back off."

"Yes, sir."

When the secretary had gone, the tall man wondered if he should have talked to the Secretary of Defense himself. What if the Russians didn't back down?

They would. The opponent had been caught on a vulnerable side. If they thought Americans to be weak, they were learning differently.

THEY ALL CAME ASHORE in dinghies, the bodies wrapped in plastic. The air was foul. The corpses smelled of the sea and of rotted flesh, and there was the smell of burned hydrocarbons from both ships and aircraft. The noise overhead continued to be as bad as it had been for hours—worse with the Harriers hovering nearby.

When they reached shore, Bishop had just brought in the Bell 222 and parked her on a flat shelf of rock near the pebbled beach.

The men had discarded the wet suits when they left the ship. They were all dressed in black fatigues. Out of habit, they had all donned commando knives and carried M-16s as if they were going into battle. Even Barrabas didn't know what the next move was going to be.

Something had changed. It was the constant whine of jets overhead. The Foxbats had turned and were winging away in the direction of Mother Russia. The F/A-18s made a triumphant sweep toward Bering Strait, then flew overhead, buzzing the 222 before heading back to their Eielson base.

The screaming of the Harrier jets had stopped. They had been recalled and had landed on their carrier as it streamed south.

The four missile cruisers circled each other like alley cats before breaking off and heading for friendly waters.

No one spoke. A helicopter landed a skeleton crew of Coast Guard sailors and took off immediately. The sailors took the dinghies out to the salvage ship. They moved the damaged ship out of sight within minutes.

A strong breeze blew in off the Arctic Shelf. It smelled of fish and seabirds again, not the pollutants of man.

Alaska had claimed her own shore and her own elements. She was whole again.

"How are you coming, Nate?" Barrabas asked.

"Finished," the computer whiz said, hunched over the radio on the Bell 222. "It doesn't look good, Colonel. Not much left of them to identify."

"Okay. Let's get the hell back to Charlie's."

They climbed aboard and were soon airborne.

"What next?" Hatton asked Barrabas over the roar of the rotors.

"It's up to the politicians. I told Jessup we'd go in if we had to," he replied.

By the time they arrived at the comfortable cabin, they were all quiet and introspective. They were fighters. Waiting was part of their way of life. But they didn't have to like it.

ALONE AGAIN IN HIS OFFICE in the rustic little cabin, the tall man broke a long-standing rule and asked his steward for a straight whisky.

Time. Time was always the tall man's enemy. He knew that his ultimatum had been effective. But it could all be for nothing. The bodies the nameless mercenaries had recovered would be useless. He'd had preliminary reports that sounded hopeless.

It's vitally important to pin it on the Russians this time, he told himself. It's not just American face, their image with the rest of the world. The enemy had attacked America and had to be exposed. They *had* to pay...somehow.

What would his people think when it all came out? His colleagues and the men and women who had voted for him? If they came up with nothing at Langley, should he send in the mercenary team to get proof some other way?

He hoped it didn't come to that. He didn't have to carry a gun. He didn't have to risk his life...not in the sense that the mercenaries did. But he would have to wait it out and pay for the consequences, whatever they were.

He was alone. It wasn't the kind of decision he could share with his wife or with one or more of his cabinet. It was all his, and he had to be right.

**19**

The mood back at Charlie's was somber. A fire burned in the stove. The log cabin smelled of woodsmoke and antiseptic.

Lee Hatton looked over the wounded Yupik and radioed for their evacuation to the base hospital at Eielson.

Billy Two and O'Toole cleaned all their weapons, test-fired them, reloaded and set aside a full complement for each SOB as if they were going into battle within hours.

Bishop and Beck checked over the Bell 222, rearmed and refueled her.

Barrabas tried to reach Jessup. The overweight Texan had pulled strings and was halfway to Washington in the back seat of a military jet.

The white-haired leader of the group returned to the table where Charlie was drinking coffee and swapping tall tales with Hayes.

From outside, the noise of a helicopter penetrated the cabin, but those inside didn't look up. It would be the men from the CIA up from Eielson to collect the

Russian bodies. Bishop had been instructed to make the delivery.

Within minutes, the retreating sound of the chopper told the SOBs the exchange had taken place. A fast military jet would be waiting at Eielson for the chopper. The CIA men and their burdens would be in Washington within hours.

All the mercs could do was wait and prepare.


IN WASHINGTON THE SUN SHONE on a brilliant May day. Tourists crowded in front of the White House or lined up for the daily tour. Inside, the President tried to keep his mind on the work at hand, knowing what was going on at Langley. It was almost impossible.

Walker Jessup sat in his apartment, an untouched submarine sandwich and a mug of beer in front of him as he stared out the kitchen window at the flow of traffic below.

For once, his mind wasn't on food. He knew what was going on in the labs at Langley. Their equipment was state-of-the-art, but it didn't look good. He had called the senator as soon as he got in, and for once, the crusty invalid hadn't barked at him. His mood was as introspective as Jessup's. They had nothing to say to each other.

Chester Good sat in the inner sanctum of his seventh-floor suite at Langley, surrounded by security, both human and electronic. When he'd taken office, it had taken technicians two weeks to satisfy his paranoid desire for total security. He had just finished calling his labs. He had called his chief of forensics at least five times in the past hour.

In the second floor labs, the forensics men had used every test they could. They had only two bodies with no histories to work on. They couldn't apply their latest techniques to other physical aspects of the dead men because they had nothing to compare them with. Their only means was to try to compare the faces and fingerprints with those on file, but the faces and hands were shredded beyond recognition.

So they sat around the lab in silence, reluctant to face the venom of Chester Good. Finally they called the DCI, who called the senator. The senator called Jessup.

Jessup still sat with the submarine in front of him, knowing he'd have to call Barrabas and not have anything but bad news for him. The fat man knew it would be like pulling teeth to get a decision one way or the other. No one wanted to send a covert team inside Russia. If they were caught, the Russians would make it sound worse than the Greenpeace deal.

He took his eyes from the window and the crowded street. He tried to think. What he needed was company...someone whose thinking was like his. He needed to bounce some ideas off someone who knew the intelligence community.

Don Fairchild. Sure. If anyone could come up with an idea, it was the old reprobate he'd worked with in the Company so many years ago.

He reached for the telephone and was soon talking to the man who had tipped him off to the interrogation of the former Greenpeace man earlier.

"So it didn't work out," Don said right away, letting Jessup know he was up to date.

"No. And I don't want to discuss it on the phone. How about dinner?"

"As I recall, I wasn't fond of watching you gorge yourself, so no gourmet restaurants, okay?" the CIA man said. "How about a beer and sandwich at Jake's?"

"You're on. See you in half an hour."

JAKE'S WASN'T CROWDED. Don Fairchild was already seated in a corner table at the back.

He was as slim as ever, but his thinning white hair and deeply lined hawklike face made him look older than his fifty-one years.

"I've ordered a corned beef on rye," the CIA man said as the waiter deposited the beer in front of him.

"I'll have a beer and a submarine. Tell them to put everything on it," the fat man said.

When they had both taken a swig of their first beer, and passed over the usual opening small talk, Jessup told Don what he had in mind.

"So they have nothing to go on but the pictures and fingerprints," Jessup said.

"That was my detail for a while," Fairchild said, taking a bite of his sandwich. "Christ! That must have been twenty years ago. It was my idea to set up a file of pictures and fingerprints of every member of the Russian staff, no matter how insignificant their jobs.''

''That was smart. Lots of KGB minor officials passed through Washington over the years, and they're top men now,'' Jessup offered.

''And lots of their people posing as minor officials at their embassy were already major KGB figures,'' Fairchild offered.

Jessup started on his sandwich, chewed the first mouthful and washed it down with beer.

''How long were you on the detail?'' he asked.

''Too long. They finally relieved me after three years. Said I was getting paranoid . . . going too far.''

''Like what?'' Jessup asked.

''I had turned two maids in the embassy—promised them defection protection eventually. Paid them well to collect little things—anything that would identify Russians we didn't know,'' Fairchild said, laughing. ''Jesus! I even had them save hair from brushes and combs. They picked up fingernail clippings from bathroom sinks. Junk bits and pieces you wouldn't believe. I remember we had a file cabinet full by the time they pulled me.''

Jessup sat, munching his sandwich and thinking. Something was nagging at him. Fairchild had told him something important, but he couldn't match it up.

The two men sat through three beers and two sandwiches. They talked of old times. Fairchild had been relieved from the boring job of checking out minor Russian officials and had gone on to bigger and better things. His successor was a plodder who never changed a routine. To this day he, or someone, was most likely saving bits of hair and fingernail clippings, as if they were important. By now, several file cabinets were probably crammed with useless bits of fluff. Both men laughed at some of the crazy things they had done for the Company. Then they went their separate ways.

IN THE OVAL OFFICE, the President mulled over the news Chester Good had phoned to him. The action taken by Barrabas's people in Alaska had been fruitless. Should they be sent in to get conclusive proof, to search the Russian base and to question other Yupiks?

Damn! He had to go for it. He couldn't let the situation stay as it was—an example of unpunished aggression.

He reached for the telephone, then pulled his hand back.

Should he send them or not? That was the question. He wished he had the guts. But it wasn't his decision. He was making the decision for almost three hundred million people, and he could be signing their death warrants. The end result could be a holocaust from which he couldn't save them.

TREE HOURS LATER, at four in the morning Washington time, Jessup reached for his telephone and dialed.

In Alaska, Nile Barrabas slept fitfully near the telephone. "Yeah?" he said, looking at the luminous dial of his watch.

"Jessup."

"It's got to be important for you to call at one in the morning."

"It is. The whole deal at Langley didn't produce diddly-squat. It's up to you." His voice was flat, emotionless, as if he was ordering eight executions.

"I was expecting this," the merc said. "I saw the corpses. No way they were going to get anything from them. I'm surprised the President came through."

"He's a gutsy guy. Glad I didn't have to make the decision."

Barrabas's brain had been working on overtime since the telephone had rung. He knew the other SOBs were awake and listening. "What's the plan?" he asked.

"No plan. Not from me. The President mentioned hitting the Russian base where they berthed the fake *Rainbow Warrior*s. The senator thought you should question more Yupiks. I think you should go for the highest ranking Russian on Chukchi Peninsula and bring him back."

The big man paused for a few seconds. "I don't like this. Jesus, if you're caught. It's not just your necks. That's bad enough. But it will look bad for all of us. Real bad."

"What's the timetable?"

"None. It's up to you."

"This time we'll do it alone. Okay?"

"Just one thing, Nile. Hold off for twenty-four hours. There's no rush. I got a feeling about this. Something could come up."

"What the hell could come up?" Barrabas asked, annoyed. "My people are itching to settle this. We're not good at sitting around, you know."

"Do it. Okay? Twenty-four hours."

**20**

In the inner reaches of the vast complex that was the Kremlin, a man sat alone in a luxurious office and gloated. His life, from childhood on, had been one long struggle to the top. But he had finally made it. It had meant being hard and daring, innovative and courageous. Just like the Greenpeace operation.

He knew both Mesmerof and Petrov had been against it—Petrov from the start, and Mesmerof when the crunch came. What the hell did it matter that people thought that the Soviets were behind it? If there was enough fog surrounding the deal, it couldn't be brought back to haunt him.

He reached for the bottle of vodka with a steady hand and poured himself the third drink he allowed himself each night. It was almost twenty-four hours since the bodies had been recovered. His informants in Washington had learned Petrov's body had been ravaged by sea creatures.

So that was it. Petrov was dead. Mesmerof was being retired. All that remained was to install Mesmerof's successor. And one more thing. Somehow, miraculously, news would leak to the Presidium about the Greenpeace project and the masterful coup. Magnanimously, the Soviet leader thought, he would have Petrov declared a hero of the Soviet Union.

Good. Excellent.

It would be another triumph.

AN ELUSIVE THOUGHT had been nagging Jessup for hours. It happened to men in his job occasionally, but never as bad as this. He knew his brain held a solution that he should be able to figure out, but it just wasn't coming.

It had started when he'd met with Don Fairchild.

The Texan was sitting at his kitchen table in a nightgown that flowed over the great folds of flesh all the way to his ankles. He didn't like sleeping naked, and he had one hell of a time getting pajamas to fit. A fresh submarine sandwich sat in front of him, half-consumed. A bottle of beer sat next to the sandwich, an inch left at the bottom.

The great jowls started to fold back in a grin. The mouth that was the entrance to the cavern that fed the monster began to split in a smile that was to last all night.

Walker Jessup, the Fixer, the man to whom the powerful came when they wanted to mount a covert operation because there was no alternative, reached for the phone and dialed a number Don Fairchild had given him.

A sleepy voice answered.

"Don. It's Jessup."

"What the hell? Don't you ever sleep, you crazy bastard?"

"Shut up and listen. We don't have much time. How well do you know the chief of forensics at your labs?"

"Well enough."

"You've got to get him out of bed. We don't have much time and the labs have a lot to do." He went on to explain the idea that had finally come to him and what they had to do.

"That's damned brilliant! What about the DCI?" Don asked, now wide awake. "Do we keep it from him?"

"No. But let him find out for himself. I've got a good idea how he'll react, and it's exactly the way I want it to go."

THE LIGHT in the President's private den was indirect, dim, complemented by flashes of red and orange flame from the fireplace where he'd ordered the fire lit after hearing from the DCI. The richly paneled walls absorbed the light and showed marvelous patterns of wood grain. The cozy room smelled of burning wood, good whiskey and the leather jackets of books.

It was past four. The robed and slippered man had taken a call and left his wife sleeping.

A phone chimed at his elbow.

"Yes?" he said.

"Mr. Good is here," an aide's sleepy voice informed him.

"Send him in."

The door was opened by a Secret Service man. Chester Good entered, his florid face, wreathed in a broad smile, instantly giving away his mood. He waddled to a chair indicated by the President. The withered strawberry that masqueraded as a nose crinkled as part of the smile.

"This better be worth getting me out of bed, Good," the tall man said, his dislike of the DCI ever evident.

"It is. The very best news. Your problem with the Russians is solved."

The President brightened.

"Several years ago, I started a program of having all Russians sent here photographed surreptitiously. I also collected fingerprints at social gatherings from highball glasses and wineglasses."

"Get to the point. We already know fingerprints and photographs have proved useless on the Russian bodies."

"I turned a couple of women in the Soviet embassy to our side. For years I've been having them collect samples of hair, nail clippings and personal objects from the bedrooms and the bathrooms of the embassy. We have quite a collection."

"So what are you trying to tell me?"

"We have lately proved that human hair has specific characteristics that are more distinct than fingerprints," Good continued.

"What the hell does it matter? Get to the bottom line, damn it." The President offered only impatience.

Chester Good wasn't affected by the unfavorable mood. He had convinced himself the coup he was about to reveal would assure him long tenure at Langley.

"I instructed my forensics people to start matching up samples of hair and nail clippings with the two bodies we recovered," he went on.

"When did you give these instructions?"

"Why, a couple of hours ago," Good replied.

"Go on," the President said. "What's the name of the Russian who guided the Greenpeace operation?"

"I'm coming to that. I told them to concentrate on men who had worked at the embassy for the past ten years. I told them to match the weight and height to the bodies...."

*"What's his goddamn name!"*

"Alexi Alexandrovitch Petrov."

"His rank with the KGB?"

"Deputy director, First Chief Directorate."

The President sat back in his armchair, relaxing for the first time in weeks, oblivious to the other man. He had them! He wasn't going to let the Russian devil go until his hairs were well and properly singed.

He gazed into the roaring flames, completely oblivious to the DCI.

He thought about men like the senator and Jessup and the SOBs, very necessary agents in the international power games a fearless superpower must play.

Lastly, he thought of the man who led the SOBs. Nile Barrabas. The last American soldier out of Vietnam. A man marked by war, in the color of his hair, in the scars crisscrossing his soul. For once, the fearless group led by him wouldn't have to be sent across that invisible line that separated freedom from slavery.

LATER THAT NIGHT, another man sat staring pensively into the flames. For a moment he was aware of his own body, sensation ending at the waist, his legs shriveled and useless. For a long time now he had blamed Barrabas for the fury of the man who had broken his spine. But he knew the truth. It had been his own fault. For a moment he felt old and worn-out.

And then the senator was glad. A potential threat had been eliminated, handled once again by a man and his group—soldiers who could accomplish the seemingly impossible. Truth shone again, while an all-out war had been averted.

Again the invalid's thoughts returned to his long vendetta. Give it up, a voice from his heart told him.

They were brave men. Mercenaries. Unacknowledged heroes in secret wars. Once again, they had saved America. The senator trembled. And silently he thanked them.

**For the millions who can't read
Give the Gift of Literacy**

One out of five adults in North America
cannot read or write well enough
to fill out a job application
or understand the directions on a bottle of medicine.

**You can change all this by joining the fight
against illiteracy.**

For more information write to:
Contact, Box 81826, Lincoln, Neb. 68501
In the United States, call toll free: 800-228-3225

**The only degree you need
is a degree of caring**